RIZZIO

RIZZIO

DENISE MINA

PEGASUS CRIME

NEW YORK LONDON

RIZZIO

Pegasus Crime is an imprint of
Pegasus Books, Ltd.
148 West 37th Street, 13th Floor
New York, NY 10018

First Pegasus Books cloth edition September 2021

ISBN: 978-1-64313-845-9

10 9 8 7 6 5 4 3 2 1

Printed in the United States of America
Distributed by Simon & Schuster
www.pegasusbooks.com

The exercises in narrative prose that make up this book . . . overly exploit certain tricks: random enumerations, sudden shifts of continuity, and the paring down of a man's whole life to two or three scenes . . . They are not, they do not try to be, psychological.

—*A Universal History of Infamy*
Jorge Luis Borges
(Preface to the first edition, 1935)

David Rizzio Plays Tennis with His Assassins

Late Saturday afternoon · 9th March, 1566
Indoor tennis court · Palace of Holyrood · Edinburgh

Lord Ruthven wanted him killed during this tennis match but Darnley said no. Lord Darnley wants it done tonight. He wants his wife to witness the murder because David Rizzio is her closest friend, her *personal secretary*, and she's very pregnant and Darnley hopes that if she sees him being horribly brutalised she might miscarry and die in the process. She's the Queen; they've been battling over Darnley's demand for equal status since their wedding night and if she dies and the baby dies then Darnley's own claim to the throne would be undeniable.

They're rivals for the crown. She knew that from the off. He wants it done in front of her.

Darnley serves to Rizzio, and Rizzio returns it with an elegant stroke. The cork ball soars across the court, reaches the far quarter and bounces high enough to land on the sloped wooden awning over the watchers' benches. There's a loud smack as it lands, rolls to the edge and falls onto the court – *plop-plop-plop*.

Point to Rizzio.

Underneath that sloping roof is a man called Henry Yair. He's watching the game, sitting on a bench built into the wall of the indoor court. He's Lord Ruthven's retainer, here to keep an eye on Darnley for the boss.

Yair hates everyone here and he especially hates tennis. Tennis is what is wrong with people. Yair is very pale, his eyes rimmed red because he hasn't been sleeping. He's watchful, sees plots everywhere. He thinks in binaries: good/bad, man/woman, Calvinist/Catholic, for God/ against God. Once fervently Catholic, he is now ferociously Calvinist. When he saw the Truth, he embraced it, and he hates those who don't, those Catholic hold-outs: how can they hold on to these broken old ideas? How can they defend a church so corrupt, so murderous, such a betrayal of the one true faith? They disgust him. He doesn't know how they can live with themselves.

Other Calvinists congratulate him on his passion, overlook the implied violence of his fanaticism, because he's on their side. The Reformation is recent, the issue undecided. It's not yet safe. Everyone is afraid of a revival of the Roman religion, of being killed for their beliefs, of spies and foreign interventions. Men as hot and spirited as Yair are useful to the Protestant movement.

Tomorrow morning, when fellow Calvinists hear that Yair was creeping around Edinburgh, when they learn what he did, who he killed, they'll all feign surprise, but in the darkness of their hearts they'll each remember his sallow face and wide watery eyes, his explosive reaction to any hint of dissent, and they'll admit to themselves that this was inevitable, that they rewarded his disquieting fervour and they've long known this could happen. Could have been any one of them stabbed in their beds. Yair was always a killing spree looking for an excuse.

From the shadows under the timber roof Yair can see the players on the bright court very crisply, the flitting nuances in their gestures and glances.

Lord Darnley and David Rizzio don't like each other but only one of them can afford to show it. Darnley sneers and looks Rizzio up and down. Rizzio keeps his expression neutral and ignores the slights. Darnley is married to the Queen and Rizzio is her servant. It's not an equal match.

Rizzio dominates as the game goes on and Darnley has to mute his intense dislike of the man or risk looking as if he's in a huff about losing. Yair watches and knows that these are courtly men. They dissemble and lie and flatter one another and, when they can't convincingly mislead, they bow or turn away to hide their faces. They're also both Catholic. They love power more than salvation. They dream of power and having power and martyring Calvinists. They serve the Pope and other foreign powers. Their loyalty is bought.

It's perishing in the indoor court. Yair's breath sparkles at his lips. He sits, arms crossed and hands tucked tight into his armpits, keeping the fingers from going numb. But thinking of Lord Ruthven's plan to murder Rizzio warms him. It warms him as if he were washed in the blood of the Lamb.

Yair eyes David Rizzio at the far end of the court. He's small and ugly and foreign. His skin looks dirty. He's crafty and sly. He's only a singer so what's he doing giving the Queen advice? The rumour is that he's a Papal spy. Yair maps every room with his sectarian dividers. He knows who is with us, who aga'n'. To justify the intensity of his disgust he suspects every Catholic of every crime he can think of. Yair was a priest, a confessor, and he, of all people, should know how obdurate Catholics think: sodomy, theft, lust, pederasty, child murder, treason both high and petty. High treason is an attack on the State; petty treason is an attack by a subordinate on a superior, usually a husband murdered by a wife. It's worse than simple murder because of the element of betrayal. It upsets the natural order of things, how God wants the world to be ordered. And in denying her husband what he wants, the Queen has become a petty treasonist.

Darnley serves to Rizzio at the hazard end. Rizzio returns the ball to Darnley and back it goes to Rizzio who knocks it out. Rizzio wins the set and smirks, trying to press the delight from his lips. Darnley scowls, turns away to the wall and lifts a sweat rag to wipe his face and Yair sees him up close. Darnley's twenty-one and handsome and arrogant. His lips are a furious tight little 'o'. He holds the cloth over his face for a long time.

Yair loves the severity of Calvinism, the purity of it. He uses it as a hook for his prickly disapproval of everything: dancing, laughing, foolishness, blasphemy, singing, food, lechery, wine, jokes, even colours – and especially fucking tennis.

⌒⌒⌒

Rizzio doesn't know they're planning to kill him tonight. He hears rumours and sees the whispering, he knows something is going on, but something is always going on: that's the essence of court life. The whispering has been intensifying for months, building up to the current session of Parliament, which will finally, irrevocably, divest the Queen's rivals of their land and power and titles. This Parliament's proclamations will take Scotland by the shoulders, turn her away from England to face Europe and concentrate power in the Queen's hands.

They're almost there.

Edinburgh is full to overflowing because Parliament is sitting. Anyone with a seat has been summoned to the capital and they've brought their households with them: families and servants, provisions, cheeses, linen, furniture, beds and their own best milking cows. All day long the ambient sound of the city is twice as loud as usual, almost deafening. At night, kitchen floors and draughty corridors are carpeted with sleeping servants and animals. Narrow streets are barely passable during the day. Everyone is on top of everyone else, watching, smiling, nodding, being seen.

Edinburgh is not short of things to whisper about.

Darnley resumes his position on the court line, holding his racquet with two hands.

Rizzio is winning this game but can't let his delight show: an errant smile tugs at the corner of his mouth. He likes to win, especially when he's playing Darnley, because he knows very well how much his rival hates to lose. Their eyes meet. Darnley can't disguise his fury; he looks away, waiting for his face to stop betraying his nature.

In fact, Rizzio has more to hide than Darnley. At one time Rizzio shared Darnley's bed, lay at his feet and called him master. He loved Darnley then and he still loves him. This yearning is his great secret, the one thing he will never tell anyone. He can hardly admit it to himself because

Darnley is handsome and rich and charismatic, but he's also a braggart and a liar, a hoormaister, a weak, weeping, drunken fool who screams demands at the Queen in public. Once he hit her at a dinner, served her a smarting slap across the face as if she were a maid come late with the wine. But Rizzio loves him. He would have served him for ever but Darnley got used to him, came to trust him and grew disinhibited in front of him. He let Rizzio see who he really was. It pains Rizzio to admit it, but Darnley is a poor prince.

It wells from one spring: Darnley's father, Lennox. A poisonous man, Lennox has turned the son against the wife, convincing Darnley that he should be on the throne instead of her. Now Darnley cannot forgive Mary denying him equal status. She promised him the crown when they married but is holding it back because of what she sees: Darnley disappearing on hunts for weeks at a time, drinking, carousing, Darnley refusing to counterseal his Queen's official documents. It's essential that he does this. None of her orders have authority without his seal added to hers and the business of government grinds to a halt when he's off on a drinking binge or a hunting expedition. The business of government is paralysed without his cooperation. They fought a war of attrition over the seal: he disappearing, Mary following him, he demanding equal status, she insisting that he earn it, until Mary upended the table. She had a copy of Darnley's seal made and gave it to her man Rizzio. Darnley seethes because of it, but the choice was never Rizzio's. He's just doing what he's told. Darnley must be able to see that.

It is pleasantly cool in the tennis court but Rizzio is sweating. His clothes are damp and his heart is hitting a steady fast rhythm. He's still fit and able and gives thanks to God for it. Good health is a rare gift at the age of thirty-two.

Darnley is slim and tall and, even at tennis, a bit pissed. He is handsome in a shallow way: his face is symmetrical, his cheeks have remarkably few craters from the pox, but he is a mealy man. The petty resentments, the bitterness, the self-pity – they all show in his eyes and pinch at his mouth. Darnley takes. No one ever leaves his company feeling better about anything. Darnley tries to make other people unhappy because he is unhappy. With a father like Lennox, who could be happy?

Rizzio sees Darnley narrow his eyes at him, raise his tennis racquet and mime serving the ball, then laugh mockingly as if he tricked Rizzio. But Rizzio wasn't tricked and hasn't moved. How can Rizzio parry this? If he mimics Darnley's joyless laugh it might look insolent. He could play along, say, 'Ha! You fooled me, sir!', but that would be patronising and Darnley can't overlook even the smallest hint of that. Rizzio could challenge him by shrugging it off, saying so what? But the moment passes, and Rizzio hasn't done anything, and he sees that that was the right move.

Remain a blank. Let Darnley roll through his moods.

When the Queen says her husband is a drunk or a waste of space Rizzio doesn't nod or roll his eyes the way other servants do. He's experienced, a professional. He knows that those he serves may deign to treat him as a friend or an equal, but he isn't. He's here because he's useful, not because he's welcome. David Rizzio makes himself incredibly useful.

He translates to and from four languages. He gives advice on drafting legislation and proclamations; he liaises with the lesser courts of Europe. He sings and makes diverting conversation. He dresses to please the eye. Mary knows how effortful this affected neutrality is: she had to learn that trick herself while she was growing up. She appreciates him for it and she trusts him.

Rizzio knows his life is threatened. Of course it is, he's a proxy for a queen. They resent her power, her sex, her religious devotion, her pregnancy which has the potential to carry on her Catholic line. They resent the compromise she represents, that there may not be a Protestant Europe, now and for ever. More than that, they hate her love match with Darnley because he's Catholic and, almost worse, a Lennox.

Darnley's family are a rare point of general agreement in Scotland: *everyone* hates them. There are not many things a rich and powerful man could do that would make everyone in the land hate them but Lennox found one:

when local lairds left the ranks of his army without permission he took their children hostage. The lairds came back but Lennox, angry at being defied, massacred eleven of the children. Noblemen's children. It was a shocking show of petty pique and animal brutality. That was twenty years ago yet half the country has still to breathe out their gasp.

But Rizzio is from Milan. He has worked in the Court of Savoy – his father was a secretary to a grand court in Italy – and he's seen far worse. 'They're all talk,' he says when he hears the rumours of threats on his life. 'The Scots threaten all the time, but they never do anything.' Nothing surprises him and, if it does, he doesn't react.

But Rizzio has not fully understood the intricate disputational customs here. In Savonese courts a coup d'état is a hot fight, a charge and call to arms. It is not preceded by months spent drawing up legally binding contracts, negotiating the spoils, redrafting, getting their secretary to read over the proposals before they sign.

Rizzio thinks that, if Darnley wanted him dead, he could run him through right here. Rizzio knows something is going on, but something is *always* going on – that's how it is in the orbit of regal power.

Across the court, Darnley lifts the ball and serves properly. Rizzio watches it come straight at him, a solid lump of cork that could knock his teeth out. He keeps his eye on it, steps nimbly to the side, swings his racquet back gracefully and meets the threat square on.

A sudden shaft of sunlight floods the court, casting a deep shadow beneath the wooden awning. Henry Yair's face is cut in half. He is nothing but lips slowly parting, seeping frost into the late afternoon.

No, You Go First

Early Saturday evening · 9th March, 1566
Mary's supper room

Mary, Queen of Scots is six months pregnant, warm and young. She is hosting a supper for her friends in a small turret room on the second floor of the James V Tower, just off her bedroom.

Every day brings her closer to safe.

Edinburgh is cold, but spring flickers at the corner of the eyes. The light has started to change: grey is giving way to blue, the days are longer, the rain feels less spiteful. The hint of renewal is echoed in Mary's body. Her breasts are full, her cheeks are flush with extra blood, her long slim body is slowly forming into an S.

New life is coming.

She doesn't know that, right now, half the nobles of Scotland are downstairs, silently storming her Palace. They are skittering around in the dark, two hundred of them, crowding the entrances and overwhelming the guards. They've already confiscated all the keys and secured the gates. At this very moment, as she raises a morsel of meat to her mouth, Lord Ruthven and his man Henry Yair are taking the stairs to Darnley's apartments on the floor below Mary's.

No one in the supper room hears anything over their kindly chat.

Mary is reflecting brightly to her illegitimate half-sister, Jean, Countess of Argyll, that Edinburgh is cold but that this is the false despair that signals the end of winter. Change is coming, good change. She grew up in Paris and there, she says, the months glide into one another. Here the change of seasons are dramatic. Jean says she likes the drama of it, the stark differences; it's easier to rejoice in the new rather than something constant and isn't awareness half the work of gratitude?

Mary likes Jean. She is bright and philosophical, an educated woman, unashamed of being clever or pursuing her interests. Lady Huntly is at the table with them. Mary is not so keen on her. She's old, and so much has passed between them that Mary can't quite believe Lady Huntly doesn't hate her. She never expresses an opinion and she never leaves Mary's side.

Mary's suite of apartments, directly above Darnley's in the tower, is a mirror of his. Both have a large formal audience chamber served by the same grand staircase, and both have a connecting passage from that room to their respective bed chambers. A private staircase joins their bed chambers so that they can visit each other without anyone else knowing: they may be heads of state but they're also a young married couple. Each of these bedrooms has two small rooms leading off into the turrets that make up the corners of the James V Tower.

Mary likes her little turret rooms. They're cosy and informal and warm, and this is where she's hosting her twelve guests this evening.

The guests with highest status are gathered at the table. Various servants and retainers stand or sit against the wall, waiting for a turn at the food.

It's Lent, and Catholics are fasting, denying themselves for the forty days leading up to Easter to emulate Christ's sacrifice, but Mary is exempt because she's pregnant. She can even eat meat. A haunch of venison is sweating in a tureen on the table and the smell of gravy fills the room. It's rich and sweet and dense. The second flank of diners, those against the wall – several of whom are not Catholic and are free to eat meat anyway – know that whatever their betters don't eat will come to them so there is an excitement in the air. There are also breads and pies and dried fruit and a warm almond milk pudding that exudes the scent of vanilla and cloves.

The room smells of love and conviviality.

Mary listens to Jean talk on the subject of gratitude, nodding as her sister runs out of thoughts, nodding still as Jean falls silent and picks at her plate. The women's eyes meet and they smile their fondness for each other. Mary flattens a hand on her belly and feels the baby quickening under her palm. A jump, a kick, a languorous stretch. She savours this moment, this small precious pocket of time when all is well, because who knows what will happen next. Maternal mortality is so common that women of means are urged to make wills when they enter their third trimester. This is why Mary is so keen to finalise the settlement in Parliament before her confinement. It'll be done in two more days. She has almost won. By Tuesday evening it'll be settled, and she can retire to have the child for whom the peace was fought.

Awareness is half the work of gratitude. Mary knows that she is warm and young and eating supper with friends. She knows that spring is coming, that they have meat and bread and health, and she is carrying a new life.

Thank God, she thinks, and she smiles and pats her stomach softly with her fingertips. Thanks be to God.

There is a companionable pause in the conversation and Rizzio fills it with a question. Everyone must answer, he says: *What is the sweetest portion of music you have ever heard and why?* And Mary smiles and drops her hand from her belly and draws a breath to answer.

This is a hanging moment in history – anything could happen . . .

On the floor below, in response to a gentle tapping, Darnley opens the door to the formal stairs and finds Lord Ruthven and his man, Henry Yair, standing there. Ruthven's cheeks are hollow and a cadaverous green, his lips thin and a strange womanly shade of burgundy.

Darnley looks at what Ruthven is wearing. 'What is that on your head?'

Ruthven reels on his heels but he doesn't answer. Behind him eighty men are creeping up to Mary's apartments. They're crouched, ordered to be silent, and holding their swords, halberds, pistols and jacks with two hands to stop them hitting the stone stairs and giving them away. No one else is dressed like Ruthven. Some of them titter at his outfit; others look annoyed, embarrassed to be led by this ridiculous man.

'Let me in,' hisses Ruthven. His breath smells of turned milk and cat piss. Ruthven, Darnley's uncle by marriage, is forty-six and has been in bed for two months, dying. Tonight his gaze is unfocused, his complexion yellowed, eyelids speckled with sweat.

Darnley admits the two men and quietly shuts the door behind them.

Ruthven staggers into the audience chamber, then just

keeps going, tripping, side-stepping over his own feet as he makes it all the way across to the passage, leading by the shoulder. He sallies on into the bed chamber, swaying and rattling softly. Yair scurries close behind, hands out as if he expects Ruthven to topple backwards.

The conspirators have nominated a corpse to lead them. Darnley is annoyed: it suggests they have no faith in the scheme and no one cares whether Ruthven gets killed. He's almost dead already and unpopular because he's so charmless. A suspected necromancer, Ruthven is just as power-mad as the rest of them but without the finesse to dress it up as religious fervour or concern for the Commonwealth. He's so unlikeable that his wife, who knows he's dying, has just formally left him. Couldn't wait another minute and no one blames her. Ruthven is an intolerable man. And he's wearing *that*. For the love of God, why is he wearing that?

Still, Darnley is young, a stranger to self-doubt, and already quite intoxicated. He decides to just plough on with the plan.

The arrangement is simple: they are to go upstairs by the private stairs, cross Mary's bed chamber and enter the audience room, unlock the main door to the stairs and let the soldiers into her parlour.

'Come on.' Darnley leads them to the tapestry wall by his bed. He sweeps the fabric aside to reveal a small doorway which leads to the narrow stairs that spiral up to his wife's bed chamber. Then he stands back to let them pass.

'No,' croaks Lord Ruthven, 'you go first.'

Darnley is surprised by this.

He shouldn't be first through the door into hostile territory. All around him he can hear the muffled noise of the men moving around in the Palace and he's not certain that Mary's company haven't heard it too. Surely he's the most important person here. He will be made King by the business of tonight and Ruthven and his man should be protecting him above all else. He most certainly should not be going first.

He motions to Yair. 'You go first,' he says.

Yair looks to Ruthven but Ruthven raises an arm in front of him. 'No,' Yair says, nodding to Darnley, 'you.'

Even Yair? Ruthven's man is more important to this scheme than Darnley?

This is how Darnley finds out that he is a pawn and not a king. The conspirators are using him. He will not be king when this is done. That was never their real plan, he thinks, was it? But Darnley's drunk and the Palace is full of soldiers and if Darnley doesn't do this his father will be very angry. It's too late to back out now.

He lifts his leg, teeters forward and takes the first step up to his wife's bedroom.

〜⚬〜

The warmth in the supper room is suddenly cut by the curtain being yanked aside. Darnley barrels in and everyone stops talking. With uncharacteristic concern for the guests, he carefully shuts the door behind him and lets the curtain fall back. That makes them suspicious. Darnley is never considerate of draughts. He walks into every room and leaves the door wide open for a minion to attend to. Ruthven told Darnley to do this. They need the door shut so that Yair can cross the bed chamber unseen and go and open the main door for the soldiers.

Mary sees Rizzio's eyebrows rise slowly and Jean's lips tighten.

In the sudden brittle silence of the supper room Darnley has an odd, vacant smile on his face. He walks across to a heavy oak chair against the wall and drags it noisily to the table, parking it next to Mary. He can't quite believe they haven't heard the army on the stairs and, still smiling and holding Mary's eye, he picks the chair up and drops it loudly. The sound rattles around the tiny room.

His smile vanishes. He juts his chin defiantly as he sits down next to his wife, then he reaches over and snakes his arm right around her waist until his hand on her swollen belly in a move reminiscent of their dancing the volte together. It's as though he's about to lift and swing her over his calf, head held high. Mary stiffens and puts her hand on his to stay it. She catches herself, resisting the urge to slap his hand away.

She breathes. She raises her chin and turns regally, three quarters on, to face her husband and lord.

For a fleeting moment they present the company with a tableau of a perfect handsome couple, milk-skinned and fine-featured, both long and slim and straight, until Darnley catches the faces of their audience. What he sees there is universal disdain and quickly averted eyes. They have no respect for him. They don't want him to be King either.

Too much has happened. He doesn't talk to the Queen or use the back stairwell at night or eat with her any more. And Mary doesn't want him here, doesn't trust him. She doesn't have enough faith in their relationship to confront him or ask him to change: she just wants him to go away. They all do.

But they are married.

Someone politely offers Darnley food but he says no, he's already eaten. They all sit in silence waiting for the lumbering interloper to do what he came here to do: have a tantrum, impart insults, make a new demand.

He squeezes Mary's waist as if being affectionate, well aware that no pregnant woman wants her womb to be squeezed, fondly or otherwise. Mary flinches and jams her thumbs under his palm, trying to loosen his grip. She breathes a tiny '*non*' and Darnley pretends he is offended that she is rebuffing his affection.

'*Cherie* . . .' he says unkindly, and suddenly every single person in the room is on edge. Darnley never calls anyone anything that isn't demeaning. Is something very bad about to happen?

Oblivious, Darnley is thinking about how sorry they'll all be when he is King. They'll all be sorry then. He'll see they are.

∞◦❧◦∞

Outside the supper room, Ruthven slumps against the bed-chamber wall. His knees are buzzing from climbing the steep steps. He's been in bed for two months and he's not getting any better. He's never felt like this before, this abiding weakness, this aching in all his joints and the strange intermittent fog in one eye. He knows he's dying. He looks up at the Queen's bed and suddenly remembers the plan — what they're doing here.

A face materialises out of the shadows at his shoulder, a long pale face that seems to glow, with wide eyes, whites visible around the pupil. Candlelight catches the texture of the bumpy, dry sclera. Ruthven is troubled that the man doesn't blink, just looks at him searchingly, eyebrows tented. It's Yair. It's his man, and Ruthven remembers afresh why they are here.

'Go!' Ruthven hisses, sweeping his hand to the passage. 'Go and let them in!'

Yair creeps across the room and opens the bed-chamber door. The corridor is only four feet long. It ends in another door which opens out into the beautifully panelled audience chamber, hung with bright drapery and furnished in velvets designed to impress visiting dignitaries. Yair has never been in here before – few have – and he steals an awestruck look as he crosses to the huge oak double doors that open out onto the staircase. He passes a cabinet of books, a trunk carved with a hunting scene, a warm fire that still throbs red in a hearth large enough to roast a pig in. A statue of Our Lady of Grace looms from the far corner.

Yair stops.

He looks at her.

The statue is life-sized, its robes gilded with gold and silver that flicker, reflecting light from the dying fire. The Madonna is so beautiful that Yair's throat aches, his dry eyes brim. For a breath-catching moment he remembers with love and shame his profound Marian devotion, how deep and utter his love for the Holy Mother once was.

Her hands are upturned in entreaty. Her head is tilted, her eyes sleepy and hooded. She steps towards Yair, emerging from the dark, a bare foot of pale glistening flesh with toes poised to take her weight. But she isn't stepping towards Yair, she's crushing the serpent writhing across a blue enamel sea. Her lips are a soft pink. Her cheeks peach. He wants to kneel before her, cleave to her, hide his sinful face in the floor.

This is what idolatry does to men.

This is the danger of the serpent's work: a wrong way, a wrong seeing, a misreading of the word of God.

Yair hurries to the doors. He can hear them shuffling out there, whispering, the muffled clank of swords and the men who will stop this sinful misdirection for ever. He spits on the shaft of the heavy iron bolt to soften the sound of metal on metal before he slides it back and pushes the massive oak doors outward. Eighty heavily armed men press in on him, shoving him back inside.

Within the bed chamber Ruthven hears the hubbub and clatter of feet on the audience-chamber floor. When he hears it he knows he's safe, that it's finally happening.

This is Ruthven's cue.

Holding out a steadying hand in case his weakened legs buckle, Ruthven clanks over to the supper-room door, wrenches it open, sweeps back the curtain inside and stands there, filling the doorway.

In a Room Full
of Razor Blades

Every face in the room turns to look at Ruthven. There are gasps and giggles. A page whispers.

What is he wearing?

He's wearing a bed shirt tucked messily into a bizarre suit of mismatched armour, missing one shin guard, with a snapped leather buckle at the side of the breast plate so it flaps about. He has a steel cap on his head. The steel cap is a deliberate, pragmatic piece of kit designed to stop someone stabbing him in the top of the head. In a courtly world where the placement of a kerchief has a special symbolic meaning, Ruthven's outfit resembles confusion screamed in high C by a panicked goat.

They all think Ruthven has lost his mind.

For one sweet moment the supper room is all concern.

Maybe he's delirious and hallucinating and has been staggering around and ended up here somehow? He doesn't even live in the Palace; he lives in a house nearby. They all know he's gravely ill and think he's in his death throes and they feel bad for him.

But Ruthven does know where he is and what he's doing. His belly aches and he's exhausted but he's taken analgesic draughts and mustered his strength. He knows this may be the last thing he will ever do and he doesn't care if they laugh. He has one foot out of this world already.

His eyes find Queen Mary sitting at the centre of the gathering. Lord Darnley, his arm around the Queen's waist in a proprietorial manner, grins up at Ruthven like a swivel-eyed loon. And there, David Rizzio sits at the far end of the table, at *the head*, as though he were the man of the house, as though he were married to her, and – this is almost worse – he is wearing a *hat* in the presence of the Queen. A bare head is the minimum of deference a servant can show his monarch, but this is a fancy black velvet cap.

Ruthven cannot credit that he could ever witness such insolence. It is so much worse than he supposed. He remembers that he has a steel helmet on but gives himself a pass. That's different. He needs it to stop his head getting stabbed.

'Oh, my good Lord Ruthven!' coos Mary. 'What is this you are wearing?'

Ruthven is still staring at Rizzio as they all register the stamps and cries of armed men piling into the chamber.

The warmth and curiosity in the room evaporates, replaced by alarm. Mary tries to stand but Darnley holds her down.

Ruthven raises a hand and loudly orders the Queen to hand over David Rizzio.

In that instant, everyone in the supper room realises that Ruthven knows exactly what he's doing: they're going to kill Rizzio. Rizzio realises this too. He is trapped and they want to murder him. Shock lifts him to his feet, and he knocks over his chair as he backs away from the door, pressing himself into the window recess.

Mary struggles to free herself from Darnley's grip, manages to stand, but Darnley gets up too, still holding her waist, which seems strange. Her fingers wriggle into his as she says, 'Lord Ruthven! David is my guest. I invited him here. By what authority do you dare order me?'

'The man is insulting you by even being in here,' brays Ruthven. His voice is too loud. He's pumping adrenaline, he's rattling with medicaments and imagines himself addressing the army next door instead of this cosy little supper party in this cosy little room.

'Insulting me? I invited him.' Her thumbs dig into Darnley's palm and she tries to push his hand off her swollen belly, but before Ruthven can even reply, Darnley turns and looks her in the eye and she knows.

Darnley's in on this – whatever this is. He's holding her pregnant body tight and he's squeezing hard, and he wants to harm her.

'It is intolerable to witness my sovereign be treated with contempt by a lowly foreigner. More than I can bear! I demand he surrender himself to me this instant!' Ruthven's voice thunders around the room, cracking off the plaster ceiling, the wooden walls and hangings.

Mary looks at Darnley, her lips parted in dismay. She's not seeing Lord Darnley, the King Consort; she's seeing her lover, Henry, the man she once spent four days in bed with, exploring, laughing with, eating from. She's seeing a man who smells of mustard seed in the evening when he's weary. She's seeing a man she once dreamed she was swallowing whole, head first, so strong was her yearning to possess him.

To *that* Henry she whispers, 'Did you bring this man here?'

And Darnley, caught red-handed, declares to the Queen and the company: 'I have no idea how he got in. I don't know what is going on or who else is involved.'

And then she feels his fingertips press viciously into the wall of her uterus. But the baby has turned and lies flush to the left side, a tiny little bottom pressing against her left forearm. Darnley is poking his fingers into vacant water.

She is confident of her baby, feels a perfect union of intent between them. She sees that her husband doesn't have the measure of her. He has no idea how far off the mark his venom lands. She holds Darnley's eye and mimics his wicked smile back at him. Darnley startles at her resolve, so much that he unhands her and steps away.

Mary looks at Ruthven. 'Lord Ruthven, as your Queen I order you to leave this chamber right now. Take your men, or I will charge you with treason.'

Ruthven looks at the food on the table, at the meat and the milk pudding and the oatcakes. He absentmindedly scratches his neck with his thumbnail.

The room waits while he recalls that he hasn't eaten today. Did he eat yesterday? He looks at the Queen. She is waiting for his answer.

Ruthven can't do anything but make it worse. He's not leaving but he isn't worried about being charged with treason either: everyone is in on this. He has a contract in his pocket, signed by all his fellow conspirators. If Mary charges him, she will have to charge four fifths of the nobles of Scotland – including her own husband.

Ruthven has two documents on him, actually; the last one was only finalised a week ago. Both are formal contracts, with clauses and sub-clauses, signatories, penalties for noncompliance, and each is signed and dated by every single man involved in this coup. They are all men, they all know Mary personally and have spent time in her company over the course of the months leading up to tonight. But Mary doesn't yet know the extent of their mendacity.

'Ruthven, get out now,' Mary commands again, 'and I will not charge you with treason. But if you stay . . .'

Ruthven looks his Queen in the eye. Everyone stands still and watches. Whatever is going on out there, Ruthven can stop this. He can call them off. He can knit the wound by backing out.

He clanks a defiant step into the room.

The room recoils at this outrage. The men stand up and go for him, but Ruthven draws a loaded pistol and cocks it – *in the presence of the Queen* – and shouts, 'I will not be handed!'

Everyone can hear the armed men shouting and clattering through the audience chamber now as Ruthven draws a dagger from his left hip, whipping it wildly across his body and lurching towards Rizzio.

Mary instinctively tries to block him, moving in front of Rizzio, but Darnley bares his teeth in a spiteful smile, and she realises how deeply involved he is.

This is when everyone else arrives.

Five armed men rush in from the audience chamber, roaring, 'A Douglas! A Douglas!' It is a battle cry from the Wars of Independence – an attempt to dignify attacking a pregnant woman in her bedroom by imagining they're at Bannockburn instead. They charge across the cramped quarters, shoving past Ruthven, grabbing for Rizzio, tumbling over one another with swords and daggers drawn.

Rizzio, terrified, flattens his back to the wall and draws his own dagger, but his hands are damp and he drops the blade. As he scrabbles for it on the floor, the men reach for him, pushing and shoving so that he staggers head-first across the room, crying 'Sauvez-moi, madame!' and darting behind his Queen.

The supper guests scatter out of the way. The table is toppled. Silver platters and goblets clatter to the floor; wine and gravy, chunks of venison and pudding splatter. All the candles are knocked to the ground.

Sudden darkness.

There are unsheathed swords everywhere.

In this dark crowded room full of razor blades the only illumination is the red glow from the fire, up-lighting everyone's face, amplifying their shadows on the ceiling and walls.

Everyone freezes.

Rizzio squeezes his Queen's skirts tight, pressing his face into the embroidery. They will surely kill him.

Mary shields him, standing tall, hands spread like the Mary of the Graces, creating a sanctuary space behind her. She has assumed they dare not come past her but abruptly sees that this is wrong. Darnley is with them. They feel protected. No presumption of authority or honour will survive tonight.

Darnley reaches for Mary with two hands as Ruthven shouts at him to look to his lady wife. *Let no ill befall her!*

Keep her well! Darnley's hands go straight for her belly. He squeezes tight, hoping to hurt the usurper inside.

That's it, My Lord! Let no ill! Ruthven is calling out these counterfactuals because he is acutely aware of the illegality of what they're doing. These statements are his defences. *I tried to protect the lady*, he'll say, *you all heard me.*

Quick-thinking Jean swoops down to pick up the single sputtering candle from the table. She holds it high above her head.

In the flickering half-light everyone can see Rizzio cowering in the window recess behind Mary, holding onto the back of her skirt. Darnley is grinning like an idiot child, both arms tight around his wife's middle. He tries to drag her away, but Mary stands her ground. She's tugging at his hands, tearful and confused, but he strengthens his hold. Everyone is watching them, wondering what sort of a man would do this to his pregnant wife. Silence. For a moment. Then pandemonium.

Ruthven brays at Darnley to get the Queen out of the way as Yair and five others lunge for Rizzio. She is set upon by unsheathed swords and daggers. They demand she give them Rizzio. But Mary doesn't move.

Ruthven shouts, 'No harm will come to him! Let him go, madame!'

Still she holds her ground, frightened but resolute, her arms spread wide, making herself bigger to give Rizzio cover.

And then a man called Kerr, John Knox's son-in-law, brandishes a cocked pistol, shoves people out of the way, and gets up close. His face is an inch from hers and he presses against her, hot breath on her cheek, as he draws his hand down her body to Rizzio's clenched fingers, touching Mary's back, arm, haunches.

With sudden horror she realises that she is no longer Kerr's Queen. He thinks she is already powerless and there will be no consequences for touching her like this.

He growls at her as he tries to prise Rizzio's fingers from her skirts, bending them back to break them. Mary may not be Kerr's Queen but she is still Mary Stuart. She stands, defiant, and Kerr cannot uncouple them until his cocked pistol brushes her belly and makes her startle. Another man unsheathes Darnley's dagger from his belt and reaches over Mary's shoulder to jab at the cowering figure of Rizzio.

The cold metal blade of her husband's dagger, held by another man, brushes her neck. A mess of invading men swarm in front of her. She feels her husband trying to squeeze the child from her and smells Kerr's fetid breath on her face. Mary knows every single one of these men, knows their histories and family connections. They would all be divested by the coming Parliament and she can have them executed for tonight.

The metal grazing her neck, the pressure on her pregnant belly, the hunks of roasted meat scattered on the floor: these are the sensations she will never forget. She will tell this story many times afterwards and she will repeat these facts, but no one else remembers these details. They don't believe them or want to hear them. They say she's making them up to gain sympathy, a charge levelled at victims by powerful men since time immemorial.

Still Mary stands her ground despite Darnley tightening his hold. David is hunkered down behind her, holding tight to her skirts, while she leans back, bending her knees to make herself immovable. Then Patrick Lindsay, a fanatical follower of John Knox, loses patience. He picks up a chair, swings it wildly and misses her belly by a hair. Mary flinches and it's enough: Darnley lifts her off her feet.

She's winded, disorientated, and when she looks up she sees that it is done. Kerr has Rizzio by the hair and is dragging him out of the room like a dog that has disgraced itself.

The last Mary sees of David is a hand taking a fistful of the velvet on his back and another grabbing his thigh. As they lift Rizzio he shouts, '*Sauvez-moi, madame! Sauvez ma vie! Giustizia! Giustizia!*' in a panic-stricken jumble of French and Italian.

Then they're out of the room with the screaming trophy, his terrified protests receding.

Ruthven slumps against the wall by the door, sweating death, and mumbles to the men that they should take Rizzio down the private staircase to the King's apartments below and to wait for him there. He'll decide what happens to Rizzio. He calls to Mary, 'Be not alarmed. We will not harm him. We are removing him from your rooms. We will not harm *you*, madam!'

'*Madame!*' shrieks Rizzio. '*Madame! Sauvez-moi!*' He's dragged across the bedroom towards the audience chamber. '*Madame! I am a dead man . . .*' This is the last thing she hears him say.

'He has been taken down to your own dear husband's chamber, madame.'

'They went the other way,' says Mary.

Ruthven doesn't understand. He shakes his head and blinks.

'They haven't gone downstairs, Lord Ruthven, they went right. They've gone into the audience chamber.'

'But I told them . . .'

This is how Ruthven finds out that he is not in charge of this coup either.

Our Queen
Is Trampled Meat

Henry Yair is standing inside the supper room as they drag David Rizzio past him to the door. He sees the wasted meat scattered and trampled on the floor, the shocked Queen over by the window. Her eyes are fixed on the empty doorway, hand slapped to her neck. Darnley is still squeezing her belly as tight as he can. He's drunk and he's not smiling any more; there's something in his face – Yair can't quite decipher it, but he fears for the woman. He thinks she might not live through the night.

Compassion betides him. A proud young woman, visibly with child, is attacked by men working in concert. *We are cowards*, he thinks, *what we're doing is wrong. The men are enjoying this. Our Queen is trampled meat.*

But then he remembers that she's Catholic and they are here to save the soul of Scotland. It is the right and godly thing to do. She gave them no choice. Empathy drains out through the soles of his feet. His doubt about what they're doing here is a splinter of ice in his heart: it melts quickly but the damage remains.

She's an unrepentant Catholic. He looks her up and down, bold, looking for things to hate. But she's comely, and her child shows through the bodice of her dress, a perfect roundel on her slim frame. She's only twenty-four and she's terrified, and her eyes flick back and forth from the doorway to the food on the floor to her drunk husband.

Yair doesn't have children. He longed to be a father. As a priest he prayed for the desire for children to be taken from him, that he might be more useful, and here is Darnley trying to squeeze his own child from his wife. But it doesn't matter what Yair thinks; he can't do anything about it anyway. Exhausted by sadness, he turns his peasant back on the frightened Queen and goes towards the noise of jeering. He crosses the bedroom to the passage and enters the audience chamber.

There he finds eighty men pressing in around Rizzio. They punch and thump him, shove and kick him diagonally across the room. The men are grinning, the candles licking up the draught from the stairs, flickering and animating the face of the Lady of the Graces. She's shocked, she's bored, she's afraid, she's laughing.

Everyone in the room has their knives out. The blades flash, spitting light around the room.

Rizzio is down. They've cornered him in a window nook next to the stairs and they crowd around him on the floor. He sees these flashes on the floor, the ceiling, the walls. He has eight seconds left to live.

Everyone has their knife out because everyone is going to stab him. That's the deal. Caesar was stabbed by all the great men of Rome. Only one of the wounds was fatal; most were just shallow nicks, tentative little gestures of implication. The collective nature of the act meant that everyone was tainted, that no one could be prosecuted because their fates are conjoined. If anyone were punished for the deed the entire class would fall.

These men are cowards.

Rizzio came here alone and he will die alone.

A blade enters his shoulder, his lung, his hand.

These men are cowards.

David Rizzio walked here from the northern shore of the Mediterranean. He saw the world and was himself. He loved a lord. He held true to his faith.

These men are grubby little cowards.

A boot hits his face, breaking his nose; there's a knife in his back, his neck.

He prays to his God, an assertion of faith, until a rough dagger is thrust into his side and the pain overwhelms him and he is suddenly blinded by a white flash of light, his body deluged by powerful sensations.

Blinded and alone, Rizzio is stabbed in the neck, the arm, the stomach and legs. Blood slides from his wounds and he's gone.

But they keep stabbing him. It takes quite a long time for everyone to have a go. Men queue up, men move forward and bend down and retreat.

This is a roll call of Scotland's great men. Great men stab and, having done their duty, they step back, make eye contact with other men. Sometimes they smile at each other reflexively as they move away, as if they're giving way at a urinal.

After the initial frenzy an eerie silence falls.

Henry Yair watches. A man pulls his knife free and looks panicked, but then he giggles as he steps away from the body. He can't believe he's allowed to do this, that he's getting away with this. Yair sees they're wilding, revelling in doing something terrible with no consequences. He knows at least some of them are thinking about the martyrs of the Reformation and hoping they are like them. But they were valiant, heroic, reckless men. This is not like that. This is pathetic.

Yair scans the room for Rizzio and spots him between the feet of the men. The shadows in the room are fluid. He sees what he thinks is the back of Rizzio's head, but someone shifts, light changes, and he realises that he's looking straight at Rizzio's bloody face.

Horribly swollen eyes that look like mouths, lips slack and bloody. As the face resolves, Yair sees the spike of an upturned quarter stave slice in through Rizzio's cheek, pass through his jaw and sink into the wooden floor below. Someone tugs the wooden handle, trying to get it back out, and the pull on the blade drags Rizzio's head off the ground, but the tip is held by the floor. The head drops back down. They try again, shaking the body with their foot, rocking the pole back and forth. The same foot presses hard on Rizzio's head, squashing his lips into a grotesque pout, and the blade finally relinquishes its hold on the floor, sliding out of his face. Legs shuffle, shadows shift; Yair cannot see Rizzio any longer.

Yair was once a priest. He gave up much to convert to the new faith but, watching this, he can't recall knowledge of God or the comfort of faith. He can't recall anything good or clean or redemptive. A heavy black melancholy cowls him – it bends his neck and turns his face to the floor.

He hears feet shuffling and grunts, metal being sheathed and unsheathed. He hears women sobbing back in the supper room, the shrill trill of Ruthven's voice. He's too sad to make out the words.

Yair shouldn't feel this way. He thought this blackness came from his fallacious faith, that God was prompting him to turn. He should be saved now. He shouldn't feel like this. Maybe God hates him. These men are not the elect. Yair is not among the elect. These men are not marked for salvation. These men are animals. He is among animals.

But he wants to believe in what they are doing, that they're doing this for a reason: to save Calvinism from foreign spies and petty treasonists who want to suppress God's truth. The Queen is the fault.

He thinks of all the ways she is culpable but it brings no comfort, so he pushes himself off the wall and stands upright. He walks behind the stabbing animal men to the grand stairs and drops heavily from step to step, falling, falling, over and over, down and down. The cold of the stone is a cleansing wash that rattles up through him until he feels that he might be dead too.

⁌⸙⁍

The supper room has emptied. Everyone rushed out the moment the soldiers left, running for whichever stairwell they could get to and leaving Mary and Darnley and Ruthven and Jean.

Mary has her arms circled around her belly to protect it. 'You brought *that* here!' she shouts at Darnley, pointing at Ruthven. 'You brought him here to frighten me, your wife, your Queen, when I am *with child*.'

Darnley sees how it looks, all the levels of wrong on top of each other, and counters with: 'You were fucking that Italian pricklet anyway. You know you were.'

'Henry,' she snaps, 'you know that's a lie.'

He does but he says, 'No, I don't.'

Mary leans in close to him and whispers so that Jean can't hear, '*Who* was *intimate* with the Italian? *Who?*' And then she tips her ear to him, pretending to listen for an answer. Darnley can't meet her eye.

'But I *did* love him,' she says, tears coursing down her cheeks. She knows what his silence means. 'I loved him for the man he was and his grace and kindness and sweetness. I could see those things because I'm not *stupid* or *blind*, and I don't trust what my *father* tells me I'm looking at before my *own eyes*. I did love David. It was not me who fucked the man.'

Jean is still holding the candle high. She pretends not to hear this conversation, busies herself toeing the broken furniture and eyeing the food squashed on the floor.

Quite suddenly, Ruthven grabs a chair and sits down.

It's a breach of etiquette, quite a major one.

He raises a hand. 'Bring me wine!' he calls, addressing a servant who isn't there. His hand drops and he slumps.

Mary takes it as a potential sign that she has been deposed but actually, Ruthven had started to fall over and styled it out by grabbing the chair. He's very unwell.

'Stand up, Ruthven,' orders Darnley.

Ruthven looks at them. His lower eyelids have come away from his eyeballs. Sweat drips from his chin. 'I can't.'

Jean gets him a draught of wine and holds the cup for him. While Mary glares at Darnley Ruthven thanks Jean with a look.

Mary is cupping her belly and shouting, 'Don't deny what you did. It'll look worse when the plan is known. You brought them here!'

'Madam, if I might?' Everyone is surprised to hear Ruthven's voice again. 'Having been husband to a lady of some strength of character . . .' Ruthven's wife is a sap. Everyone knows it. She's nice but stupid; she wouldn't have married him otherwise. 'My own lady is sometimes of a mind to disagree with my own good self.'

'Oh no . . .' mutters Jean in a flat voice.

Ruthven rambles on. 'A wife must listen to her husband and give him obedience. Is it not in the marriage vows: to love, honour and obey? If so, is it not a contravention of the wedding contract to disobey? And in this way is it not the case that the marriage cannot be said to be a continuing conjoining if the wife is disobedient? Abeyance to her husband being central to the contract and the wedding vows being sacred? It is God's will that, if a woman defies a man, they must be divorced in the eyes of God. Has not God said so?'

Mary is listening now because of the implication. The suggestion that she is not married is a direct threat. Her baby must be born into a valid marriage and must be admitted by Darnley as his. Otherwise it will be denied the security of the throne. Without those seals, even if the baby makes it to the throne, it will surely be usurped, and that always leads to murder.

But what Ruthven is saying is legal nonsense. Mary looks to Darnley to refute the point, to say she is his wife, that this is his child, shut up, Ruthven. Darnley doesn't.

Darnley is Lennox's son. He tried to lift her by her belly to make her miscarry. He is going to hold her belly hostage, withhold an admission of paternity to get the crown. He's a Lennox. She remembers all those nights when they would whisper quietly and he would say, 'Save me from them, sweet Mary. Save me from this family of mine, this nest of vipers, this yoking sophistry, save me sweet Mary.'

He is his father's son and nothing is beneath his spite, not even infanticide.

Henry Yair Meets His Gallows Twin

*O*i!

Yair is walking out through the front gate when someone grabs his sleeve.

'Where do you think you're going?'

Yair looks up. Five of the new guard, their own men: he can tell because their clothes are mismatched and home-made and the weapons crude. He points up the hill. 'Town.'

'You allowed to leave?' The men look back and catch the eye of the officer in charge. He's taller than them and his nose is so flat that the bridge of it seems to cleave inward to his skull. It's Sheriff Thomas Scott, Ruthven's man from Perth.

'You know me,' says Yair, surprised to find his voice is low but steady. 'I'm Ruthven's man too.'

'Oh aye.' Scott's about to wave him off but stops, looking past him to the city.

Lights are appearing – first one, then another, then five or twenty – and they're coming straight for the Palace gates. The men of the City of Edinburgh, four hundred citizens, walk in formation, carrying torches that form a river of fire.

These are the ordinary men of the town who have sworn to keep the peace, called from their beds by the Keepers of the Watch. Strange goings-on had been noticed down at the Palace: lights on and shadows slamming into windows, armed men hanging around the gates. The townsfolk had watched and seen and sounded the alarm. Provost Simon Preston is at the head of the Keepers. It was he who mustered the men, got them to arm themselves and leads them now, marching towards the trouble. They are all of a single mind, armed with lances and torches, fuelled by fierce loyalty to Queen and Government and Civic Order.

The river of fire pools in front of the entrance to the Palace. The guards step forward from their posts. They can see that the Keepers are not men to mess with.

Simon Preston raises a hand and the men behind him stop. They stave the end of their lances on the ground and the clatter makes Yair's teeth ache.

The guards stand stiff and nervous but Yair is pleased in a way. He thinks the Keepers of the Watch are going to find out what they have done here tonight. He thinks they might charge them and kill them and he's half glad that it'll all be over. He sees Preston look up to the Queen's apartments and the window of her bed chamber. Preston knows the Queen is embarking on her dangerous third trimester, straddling life and death. Preston's own wife has had nineteen live births. He knows it's a time of great danger.

The façade of the James V Tower is only about fifty feet broad with a turret at each corner. In between the turrets, facing outward, are two big windows, one above the other: one for the Queen's chambers, the one below for the King's. These are the biggest windows but there are smaller ones in the turret walls.

Preston tells Scott that something was seen to be happening in the Queen's apartments: sudden movements, lights going on and off, someone falling against the glass. He didn't see it himself but several of the Keepers here present were told by people who did see it. It might all be hearsay but he wants to know what's going on, and now they're all here he can see that the men are not Mary's official guards. He doesn't recognise any of them.

The Queen's rooms are brightly lit.

Preston shouts up at the window, 'WHAT'S HAPPEN-ING IN THERE?'

'It's nothing,' says Scott. 'Everything's fine.'

'These men . . .' says Preston. 'I know most of the guard but I don't know any of these men. Who are you?'

'Just filling in,' says Scott, 'It's fine. You can all go home.'

'Aye?' Preston looks at Scott's nose and hears his out-of-town accent. 'Where is this you're from?'

'Up Perth way,' says Scott. 'I'm Sheriff up there, by Lord Ruthven.'

'Ruthven . . .' says Preston, knowing Ruthven is a bad lot, that the rumours are he's a necromancer, and, whether you believe that stuff or not, it means there's something odd about him. 'I see. How come you're guarding the Palace? That's not for you to do.'

Scott doesn't answer. He doesn't seem to know what to say. The pause goes on too long.

Someone behind him clears their throat. Someone else drops his lance and it clangs loudly on the cobbles. The sound ricochets off the brickwork of the Palace and everyone notices suddenly how quiet it is. Normally there would be movement and people and horses and carts.

Grips tighten on lances among the Keepers. Feet shuffle and scrape as men part their legs to steady their stance.

Preston looks up at the James V Tower again and sees all the light spilling from the windows in the Queen's apartments and the King's below.

'Aye . . . see,' he says, 'but to *us* this seems kind of strange. You're not the usual guard, eh?'

Scott doesn't answer. He smiles vaguely and looks over his right shoulder, mapping his men from the corner of his eye.

A moment's pause.

Preston advances and raises his left arm. He gives a nod and the men behind his left flank shuffle forward. Preston raises his right arm and the men on that side do the same. Both sides are now spread out in a semi-circle, curved around the gaggle of strangers on the door.

The shuffling stops. Preston calls the order and the Keepers drop their lances, blades pointing at these unknown guards.

Simon Preston looks up at the Queen's apartments and shouts, 'IS THE QUEEN IN THERE?'

No!

Darnley has stopped pretending someone else let Ruthven in. He is annoyed now, because Mary won't stop being angry about it and it wasn't even his idea. They've moved into Mary's bed chamber and they're sitting at her escritoire under the big window. Ruthven is apart from the group, slumped on a chair outside the supper-room door. He asks for more wine and Darnley tops him up. Mary is watching the guards at her door, two men who are both unknown to her, blinking awkwardly and trying to hide their faces. There are others in the room but these two are afraid.

She gets up and goes towards them, sees them turn away, and sits on her bed to pretend she was not going towards them, was not trying to see their faces.

This is when they see the Keepers' lights.

They see the glow of a hundred torches coming down the hill towards the Palace. At first, they can't see the men, just the flickering on the buildings around them, eating into the dark night sky. It intensifies – it's definitely coming down the hill. The noise of the men's feet bursts out of the narrow street and into the quadrangle in front of the Tower. The torches are so bright that in Mary's room it's suddenly midday at the height of summer.

Hope. In Mary's bed chamber everyone stills and listens. Ruthven drops his cup.

Mary hopes that the Keepers will somehow realise what is going on and break in, that the good people of Edinburgh, her loyal subjects, will free her.

She stands by the foot of her bed and listens to the exchange between Preston and Scott. She maps the room: Ruthven sitting, Darnley over by the door to the audience chamber, Lady Huntley near the supper room. Three guards are blocking the exits: one on the private stairwell, two by the audience chamber. They watch her reaction to the furore outside.

Mary's face turns to the window; her lips part as if she is going to take a breath and call for help. The nearest guard raises the tip of his sword to her chest as he leans forward and hisses, 'Lady, call out or make a single sound, and we will cut you into pieces and throw you from the castle walls.'

Mary regards him. She's remembering his face and he sees that. He drops his sword. His impertinence lacks conviction. This is the first time she has seen a faltering, and she knows that this may be her moment.

From outside they hear the provost shouting up to the window, 'Is the Queen in there?'

It's the right question.

Ruthven looks at the guards. The guards look at the window. Mary has the support of her people; they love her, and if Preston and the Keepers get in here the guards will all be killed. Ruthven will be killed. His estate will be taken, his titles confiscated.

Darnley comes alive, steps over to the bright window and throws it open. He hangs out like a washerwoman and shouts down at Preston, 'Hello!'

'Oh!' Preston is delighted to see the King. 'Hello!' he replies. 'I'm Provost Simon Preston. I'm the Keeper of the Watch.'

'Good for you,' says Darnley, smiling and looking over the arc of lance-bearing men pointing their weapons at the Palace Guard. 'What's going on here?'

'We thought we heard trouble,' says Preston.

'Oh, you did! We found a Papal spy. Two of them. They tried to get away, but we've caught them and dealt with it all. Had to put extra guards on, just in case there were outside agents. A trusted servant, as well – imagine! Creeping around, sending word back to Rome. Had letters on their person that proved they were passing information and plotting . . .'

Darnley is giving too much detail, a sure sign of a false story, and all to a subordinate. This makes Preston wonder if he's being fobbed off, but what can he do? Darnley is married to the Queen. He can't very well question him.

'Oh,' says Preston, smiling up but still not convinced. 'Fancy that.'

'Yes,' says Darnley. 'So . . . you can all disperse and go home now.'

This doesn't feel right to Preston. He doesn't want to leave but he's being told to by the King Consort from the window of the Queen's apartments. What else can they do?

He turns to the men and orders them to go back to their homes, thanking them for their service. The men turn and clatter away, making their way back to town.

Darnley remains at the window, smiling stiffly and watching them leave, which Preston again finds out of character. Darnley is known for being a snobby, surly little shit.

Preston lingers. He wants to make certain that everything is done in good and proper order. If they did find a spy in the Palace tonight, he wants the Keeper to be spoken of well at the trial. He lets the men get well ahead of him and checks that the quadrangle is clear. And then he hears the window being shut behind him, and as it closes, he hears a woman's voice calling one word.

'No!'

The intonation rises. Was it a cry? Is it a cry? Was it the Queen? He turns to look up at the bright window. He looks at the guards but they don't seem to have heard anything. It wasn't very loud. He glances up again, expecting a shift in the light or a movement. But there's nothing.

Provost Simon Preston goes home and lies in his bed. He blinks into the dark, replaying that single plaintive syllable. He might have been mistaken. Could he have heard something else and imagined it was a voice? He hears it over and over until he can't make sense of it any more or think about anything else.

John Noir, Papal Spy

Yair joins the Watch and walks into town amidst the throng. He's standing near Simon Preston as they leave the quadrangle and he, too, hears the squeezed little cry of 'no!', but it doesn't haunt him. He's already so mired in despair that nothing can penetrate his mood. Nothing touches him, not the cold or the chattering camaraderie of men returning home after a false alarm.

The men peel off, left and right. They are nibbled away by the city, swallowed by doorways and closes and lanes until they are very few. Those who are left decide to go for a drink together and talk over what happened tonight. They walk fast, looking for somewhere open. It's late. Yair drops back until he's at the very back of the group and then slides away, unnoticed.

He walks for a long time, stuck in a half-thought. He heads up to the Castle and then down to the houses below.

He circles the foot of the Castle, walks the lower levels of the dark city, down through the lanes to the Grassmarket, the undercity, following his own feet. He doesn't mean to go anywhere in particular, just walk until he's exhausted, but he finds himself outside Father Adam Black's front door.

Adam Black is notorious.

He's everything Henry Yair isn't. He's a forty-year-old Dominican friar, well-off, cheerful, lascivious and much travelled. He's been all over Europe, once all the way to the Holy Land. He is sympathetic to the transgressions of those who come to him for confession because Black is a sinner himself. He's suspected of being a spy. It's rumoured he reports to the Spanish, he reports to the French, he sends missives to the Vatican in cypher. His spy name is 'John Noir': that is what they call him in their letters by return. *Ask John Noir if* . . . *Tell John Noir to seek* . . . *Must John Noir find* . . . Everyone in Edinburgh knows these facts. Black is only tolerated because he's not often in the city, and when he is it's never for long. He was chaplain to Mary of Guise, the current Queen's mother, and his official status is murky now.

Adam Black's front door is small and pale blue with a large brass knocker brightly buffed. His house stands alone on a patch of land that backs onto Greyfriars cemetery. Yair thinks he has been brought here because he desperately needs to talk about matters of faith. He wants to know if his chest should hurt like this, if he has been mistaken in his conversion. He wants to ask why God is making men choose between religions like this when they can't. They don't know. They're gambling their immortal souls. Yair can see both sides of the argument. He's guessing now, but this feels like an answer of sorts, finding himself here at a priest's house.

God shouldn't ask men to answer these questions.

Yair looks at Adam Black's door, wants to go in, but the house is in darkness. Still it is a sign, finding himself guided here. He tries the door. He has never done that before. In these porous moments, every tiny thing can take on significance and be read as a sign from God. The door yields. The bolt was not properly pulled. Henry Yair steps from the street into Father Adam Black's parlour.

He wants to do the right thing, make the right choices. It's a gamble. He saw Rizzio's face cut through with a blade. Eyes like lips.

Then he's standing by a bed, in a small room, a stifling room that smells of wax and old men's clothes, and Yair finds himself smiling. He doesn't have to decide. It's been done for him.

He's holding a knife he's never seen before, holding it in his right hand which is covered in blood. It's warm blood and it's dripping onto the floor in a way he finds amazing. The blood of the Lamb. He is washed.

He doesn't have to decide anything any more. It's all been decided for him.

A woman is screaming words. It's Father Black's sister and housekeeper. She's screaming words close to Yair and then far from Yair, and then men are here.

Men make him drop the knife and men hold his arms, and they light candles and see Father Adam Black in his scarlet soggy bed, and he has been stabbed over and over in his lovely holy face.

Strange Noises in a Familiar Space

Night has fallen in the Palace and Mary is trapped. She is fully clothed, sitting on the side of her bed in her emptying chamber, ordered to retire by Ruthven. Everyone is leaving. She still doesn't know for certain that Rizzio is dead but she thinks he must be. She heard laughter and cheering from her audience chamber and now it has gone quiet out there. She looks at Darnley and Ruthven.

Darnley comes over and tells her to cooperate. Then he goes away again.

Ruthven clunks over and tells her the baby will have no father if she divorces the bairn's father by defiance before it is born.

Jean, who has never left her side since supper, catches

her eye, and Mary can see her mouth twitching and her eyes saying: look at this daft old fool who doesn't even understand how bastards are made. A bastard is conceived out of wedlock, not born.

Ruthven keeps sitting down in her presence, another impertinence, and Darnley leans over to talk to him in low tones. They look around furtively — it's pathetic — not wanting her or anyone else to hear what they're saying. Her husband is an imprudent idiot. He's going to get them both killed.

Lady Huntly comes in. She's been allowed to take out the broken crockery, to tidy up and straighten things.

She approaches Mary and looks at her intensely.

'David?' asks Mary.

Lady Huntly glances back to the audience chamber.

'Out there?'

Lady Huntly nods and bows her head sadly.

There is no noise coming from the room. Mary looks to Lady Huntly, imploring her to say it isn't true. But it is, and they both know that.

Lady Huntly does an uncharacteristic thing now. She puts her hand on Mary's wrist; it is less of a caress than a brief transfer of heat from an old body to a young one, and she snorts through her nostrils, loud as a horse.

'God rest his soul,' she says.

Mary looks at the door to the passage. David is in there, and if David is in there, David is dead.

David Rizzio walked most of the way from Nice to Edinburgh. It took him three months. He came in the diplomatic train of the Count of Moretta, sensing that the Scottish capital was a place where a fortune could be made. He didn't come from a rich family, but his father spent all his money on education for David and his brothers, and it showed. He was the smartest man Mary ever met, chic in his dress, pretty in his manners, and he could sing so well that the other choristers called him *David Le Chant*. She always knew David loved Henry. She saw the way he looked at him, eyes tracing his profile, the turn of his soft chin, the wonder of his well-turned leg. David saw what she saw in Darnley: his ethereal beauty and cruelty, the pettiness and the grace.

Lady Huntly sees that Mary understands. She pats her wrist and lifts her empty basket, goes into the supper room and noisily gathers spoiled food and smashed plates.

Lady Huntly, née Elizabeth Gordon, is fifty-three, old enough for no one to look at her. She was married to Scotland's richest man, George Gordon, Earl of Huntly, but he died of a stroke on the battlefield fighting against Mary.

Lady Huntly was made to attend his posthumous trial for treason, at which his embalmed body was propped up and adjudicated over by the full Parliament. At the same trial Lady Huntly's seventh child, her son John, was condemned to be executed on the Queen's orders. Giving

Lady Huntly a position among Mary's ladies was supposed
to be a sign of the Queen's clemency. But part of the
embalmed Earl of Huntly's punishment for rising against
her was the forfeiture of a great many furnishings and
tapestries and wall-hangings, velvet padded beds, and gold
and silver ware. All of those things came here, to Holyrood
Palace. Lady Huntly sees them all every single day as she
waits on the Queen, these remnants of her past life when
she wasn't a widow and her son John was still attached to
his head. Every moment here is a penance. She comes out
of the supper room with a basket of broken things and the
guard at the door lets her out.

Mary watches her leave. She sits down on the bed and
cradles her belly. They're going to kill her tonight. Once
they've built up their courage, once they've discussed it
and sorted out the ramifications, they'll try to kill her and
then Darnley. It's the prudent thing to do. It's what she
would think to do. She needs to stop this.

Darnley comes and sits next to her. He looks chastened.

She whispers, 'Is our David dead?'

He shrugs a stupid shoulder because he knows he is
dead. He's just too cowardly to admit it.

Across the room, Ruthven gets up. He's exhausted, and
his armour is heavy and he staggers a little, but he catches
himself and then raises a hand to Darnley.

'Go down,' he says, sweeping an arm from Darnley to
the private staircase.

At first Darnley thinks he is delirious. He snorts and looks at Mary for confirmation that she saw Ruthven give him an order.

Mary tips her head. What do you expect? she thinks. You're a hostage as much as I am.

'Let's go downstairs, Lord Ruthven,' he says loudly, as if it was his idea all along, but Ruthven is already rattling across the room to the staircase.

As Darnley passes her, Mary reaches out and grabs his forearm: it's as intimate as she can bear to be with him right now.

'Stay with me tonight?' she whispers.

He knows she wants to try to convince him to turn back to her side. He smirks at her and pulls his arm away. No, he says, and takes a step beyond her towards the stairs.

She whispers so quietly that only the two of them can hear it: 'They'll kill you too.'

But Darnley walks away, through the doorway and down the stairs and she doesn't even know if he heard her.

She bolts the door behind him but it's symbolic. The guards are still in her audience chamber. They won't let her out of this room.

Mary is left sitting on her bed as all the lights die away. Lady Huntly's duties now should be to help her undress. When they know they are alone she comes over to her Queen and sits on the bed next to her, thigh pressing to thigh, and takes her hand. They listen to strange noises in the familiar space. Doors closing, feet on stairs, yells in the quadrangle, the rumble of voices below.

The two women hold hands, and Lady Huntly weeps silently. Mary doesn't weep; she can't relax enough for that. But she doesn't withdraw her hand. They sit there for a long time.

Dancing on the Lip
of a Lion Pit

I n a distant room across the Palace two men in their early
thirties are finishing a meal, telling old stories, gossiping
and drinking. They're both connected to Lady Huntly:
George is her son and James is her new son-in-law, married
to her daughter less than three weeks ago. They've been
there for hours, enjoying one another's company, talking to
see the night through, oblivious to the coup.

These are genuine friends.

Unusually for the period, their friendship never feels
transactional or ceremonial. It seems authentically fond:
being together changes them. When they're together they
are braver and more reckless than they are alone. They find
things funny. They change one another's minds. They act in
concert.

James Bothwell is famously unclubbable, an honest shit who won't take bribes, but he's also an adulterer, an adventurer and a rapist. George had to watch his brother's execution, his father's corpse tried for treason and, just like his mother, he walks past the spoils of his family's defeat all day every day.

Both men work closely with David Rizzio and give the Queen their counsel. They're both very loyal to her. These are circumspect times: the ruling class is very small and, essentially, you can pick and choose who your enemies are because almost every house has done something awful to someone else.

They're laughing together at something when they hear the banging on the door of their chamber, so loud and formal – KNOCK! KNOCK! KNOCK! – that it makes them laugh even more. They think someone is playing a joke.

'Enter!' calls George in a sombre bass.

'*Entrez!*' shouts Bothwell in an affected French accent.

They both gawp as a servant opens the door from outside to reveal their caller, Lord Ruthven. He stands in a full set of armour, ruddy-faced, puffing hard from climbing the stairs in all his metal, and he's wearing some sort of bizarre steel cap with a leather strap that buckles by his ear. James knows not to laugh in his face. They pity him. The man is dying, everyone knows, and he has no sense of humour, much less a capacity for self-deprecation.

James stands up to greet him, inviting him into the room, but George, the giggliest of the two, has to bow very low, doubling over so that Ruthven can't see him struggling not to laugh. They're both quite drunk.

Ruthven clanks into the middle of the room and collapses in a chair, listing to one side as if his armour is digging in. His expression is careworn and distracted. They are courteous, though, and offer him wine and a stool for his feet.

'Lord Ruthven, how nice to see you out and about again.' This is George, who is the kinder of the two. 'Could I offer you a cup of wine?'

Ruthven sighs. 'Look, we have taken over the Palace, we have killed Rizzio and taken the Queen hostage. Tomorrow we'll dissolve Parliament and restore the exiled lords. Everyone knows and everyone is coming back. Most of them are already here, hiding in town. The Queen, who you have been grooming and kowtowing to all this time? She's out.'

He shifts in his seat, seems to forget what he's talking about.

George pours him a cup of wine and hands it to him. 'Lord Ruthven, is the possibility of a treason charge something that concerns you?'

'No.' Ruthven drinks, still looking vacantly into the fire. 'There won't be a charge. We've got Darnley.'

'Oh.'

George suddenly feels terribly sober. He looks at Bothwell. Bothwell is watching Ruthven and nodding. He's not agreeing, he's just hiding what he really thinks.

This is a disaster for them. James and George had plans. Darnley is a spoiled child. They never even bothered counting him among the pieces on the board.

'We've promised him the Crown Matrimonial,' puffs Ruthven. 'So he'll basically do what we tell him.'

George sits down and leans forward, hands on his knees, elbows sticking out at belligerent angles. A nervous smile crackles on his face. 'He's a rather changeable person, my Lord Darnley, though, isn't he?'

Ruthven puffs his burgundy lips in agreement.

'Aren't you even a little worried he'll change his mind?'

'No,' says Ruthven. 'We're golden. He signed a contract ordering us to do all of this. We made it seem that we were following his orders. But I don't want you two to worry because you're all right with me. I'll see to it. Don't be alarmed.'

George makes a little cooing noise that suggests he's impressed, surprised but impressed, and well done. And then he says, '*We* being . . . ?'

Ruthven looks at him for the first time. 'Me. Us. The Lords of the Congregation. The Chaseabout Lords.'

George nods as if he's struggling to understand. 'The Chaseabout Lords who rose in objection to Darnley and Mary's marriage are now holding the Queen hostage until

Darnley gets the Crown Matrimonial?'

'No. He gets the crown, and they get their lands and titles restored.' Ruthven knows it doesn't really make a lot of sense. Even if there is a contract, even if everyone gets what they want, they need a principle to justify what they're doing, a natural law principle that makes the desired outcome seem noble and somewhat more righteous than a simple brigand's demand.

'Because a queen is an offence to nature?' suggests Bothwell, helping him out.

'Yes!' says Ruthven wagging a finger at him. 'Yes, the second sex! A trumpet cry and so on. A king is what we need.'

'Quite so,' says George, unconvinced and thinking about Darnley.

'*Just* so,' says Bothwell, half smiling at Ruthven.

Ruthven feels a bit confused now and tries to get up but can't. George jumps to help him, using the old method of getting a nobleman in armour up from a chair: he stands on Ruthven's metal-covered toes and holds his upper arms, using his own weight to lever him up. This makes Ruthven nostalgic, and he grins and says he hasn't seen that done in a long time. George says he used to do it for his father; he and his brother used to take an arm each.

Then they mill around in the middle of the room, smiling as each remembers other times and older ways until Ruthven very abruptly says he has to leave.

'Well, thank you very much for coming to tell us,' says George at the door, and they all shake hands.

Ruthven clanks off down the corridor to tell Lord Atholl he isn't going to be murdered either, nor will the other Mary loyalists, and Bothwell shuts the door.

The two men stand behind it.

'It's Lennox behind this,' says Bothwell quietly.

'How do you know?'

'Lords of the Congregation are run on English money and, with Darnley at the head, it's got to be.'

George and Bothwell don't hate Lennox for any moral reason. Their beef is Europe or England. The Lords of the Congregation, the Protestant reformers, want closer ties with England to cement their religion but Bothwell and George, while Protestant themselves, know that an allegiance with England will dilute their power. European ties, however, would bring less money but fewer obligations. No one in Europe really cares about Scotland; they just want to mess with England. European ties mean Bothwell and George Huntly will be better able to exert control here.

'They all know we're loyal to her,' says Bothwell.

'Hmm.'

'It isn't within Ruthven's power to grant us mercy.'

'I know.'

There was a time when Ruthven would have worked this out himself, and it's a little embarrassing that the old beast came lumbering into their room trying to grant clemency when what he was really doing was warning them.

George excuses Ruthven with a shrug. 'He's dying.'

Bothwell nods kindly. 'I see that. He'll go back up and tell the others he came to see us. Then they'll realise that they'll have to kill us.'

'Yes, they will.'

⁓

James and George stand still in the darkened room, listening. The soundscape in the Palace is unfamiliar. It's busy and chaotic compared to the usual orderly night guard.

The invading soldiers are all over the Palace, elated by their win. They're sitting on chairs and rifling through the kitchens, taking anything that isn't nailed down, wrestling each other in the throne room. There's no discipline. It bodes ill for the rest of the night. They can't escape through the main doors, and the only other way out that either of them is familiar with is through this back door. They can see the small, shuttered window at the far end, a semi-circle of muted grey moonlight. They can hear the guard but don't know if they're outside or upstairs.

They listen but they can't map what they're hearing. It tells them nothing about who is coming or going. There is no order. Finally, James shrugs at George, points at the window and goes towards it. George follows, eyes trained on his friend, expecting a door to burst open, a troop to arrive, swords to swing, a cry of alarm to go up, but no one stops them.

They lift the shutter, open the window, and James slithers out easily. George is less graceful, and James has to pull him through by the arm.

They stand outside in the Palace garden in the dark. Their eyes meet, the cold pinches their cheeks. Suddenly they hear feet tramping in unison nearby – not necessarily coming for them, just marching sounds. But they're full of adrenaline, and they take it as a cue and they bolt.

They sprint over lawns and through rose bushes, past seats and high hedges, clamber up and over a walled enclosure, silent and swift. They're remembering being young and being fast, and, not yet out of breath, they feel invincible and joyous running together, young bucks running with terror at their back and courage ahead.

The moon comes out and sudden detail crystallises: silver dew on blades of grass, the flashing eyes of a mouse startled still, Bothwell's eyelashes, George's freckles.

They speed up, racing each other for the joy. Neither of them will ever feel this strong again.

Bothwell sees something on his right and gives a yip of delight. He peels away from his running mate's side and heads towards a low wall.

It's the lion pit.

Holyrood keeps two mangy lions in an underground cell. The pit is a wide circular well used to view the scrawny creatures from above. The brick walls amplify their roars and make them seem more frightening than frightened.

James leaps onto the low wall and skips along it, dancing and grinning back at George. George laughs silently at his crazy friend, still running, turning when he overtakes, running backwards so he can stay watching Bothwell for longer.

And the Earl of Bothwell dances a jig on the lip of a lion pit in the middle of the night.

Great Men of History,
Foiled by the Mean

All night, the major players are gathered in Darnley's audience chamber. Darnley's father, Lennox, has appeared. He is there with Ruthven, Morton and all the lords who were overlooked and sidelined by Mary.

These men are all landed aristocracy. They're all white, between the ages of twenty and sixty, and, literally, entitled. These are the men who fill history books with their squabbles and claims and resentments. The Great Men of History.

These men know they are great. They feel confident that they have just changed the course of history with their forcefulness and righteous vigour. They haven't. Their plans will be usurped by a dumpy widow-woman carrying a piss pot.

But for now, these insurgents sit in Darnley's audience chamber imagining themselves seen through the prism of time: great men standing up for each other, preserving their estates and turning Scotland to Calvinism. Lennox courted Mary's mother in her widowhood but was rejected. He courted Mary but she was having none of it. He's a power-worshipping, child-murdering pragmatist who can't even commit to a side in the Reformation. He's somehow Protestant enough for Henry VIII but Catholic enough for Bloody Mary.

Lennox dominates the conversation. He says less than everyone else yet every turn in the debate is driven by him, every decision set up by his few words.

He is tall, like his son Darnley. A long man, thin of body, slightly withered about the face. He fed Mary his idiot son and now he's working him from the back. Persistence has paid off.

He can hear her pacing in her bed chamber upstairs and tells the company, 'That's the problem.'

'That's a *problem*,' says Ruthven.

'Like Rizzio,' says Lennox. 'A problem. Her *and* Rizzio's baby.' He smiles and nods to his cuckold son, who knows he is not a cuckold. Darnley smiles back, thinks there is nothing worse than his father smiling. No good has ever come of it.

'Yes, but we wish the lady no harm,' says Lord Lindsay, who is always the weak link. He's standing in the middle of the room, a short, stubby man who does not take wine and no one knows why. He's never drunk, and it makes him seem peculiar and annoying. 'We will hold her and the baby prisoner in Stirling Castle.'

'For how long?' asks Lennox, letting Lindsay find the flaw in his own cloth.

'As long as need be,' says Lindsay.

'How long is that then?'

'Certainly for the rest of their lives if necessary. She'll like it there. She can nurse it and go in the yard for exercise and shoot her new bow and do embroidery. That is *fitting*.' And so Lindsay witters on, never cutting a thought short or wondering why, among all of these great men of the world, he alone is holding the floor. The rest of them know better than to talk too much.

'So we will not kill her,' says Lennox, apparently concurring.

'That is decided,' says Lindsay.

'But what if the lords who have been visited by Lord Ruthven and let go this evening come back and try a counter-coup? Take the Queen from us and use her as their head?'

'You mean if Stirling Castle is not secure enough? What then?'

'Yes.'

Lindsay makes a sad face and glances at Darnley. 'I can't say . . .'

Darnley isn't going to either. He pours himself a drink and turns away. Will they imprison him in Stirling Castle too? If they kill Mary will they kill him? Even his father being there is no guarantee that they won't. Lennox wouldn't hesitate to allow his own son's execution if it were expedient. Darnley knows that.

'And if she bears a boy . . .' says Lennox, talking about his own grandchild.

'Oh no, it'll be a girl,' says Ruthven. 'I know it. I know the signs. There's no threat in letting the infant live. So we won't kill it. That would be improper.'

Thus Lennox and Morton and Lindsay all agree that they should not kill Mary or the baby because it's only a girl and Stirling Castle is secure. Their cold eyes dart to Darnley. Definitely.

'An Italian girl,' muses Lennox, already developing a defence.

Mary is carrying Darnley's baby. He knows that and so does Lennox. Darnley knew Rizzio. He had Rizzio many times. Darnley likes boys and girls, but Rizzio didn't, and the baby Mary is carrying was conceived at the very start of their marriage, when Mary was infatuated with him. She adored him. 'The best-proportioned long man I ever saw,' she said of him. Darnley knows it's his child they're deciding not to kill, and he does care, but only in as much as the suggestion slights him. Not one iota more.

His father gives him another crooked smile. Darnley

reciprocates. He may be drunk but he can see the other men's hooded eyes and half smiles; he knows they don't respect him. And Ruthven and Lindsay are sitting down again in his company, he realises. They haven't even asked his permission.

Just then, Morton, the second man to Lennox, saunters into the audience chamber, without permission or invitation, as if he owned the place. Everyone in the company startles at the breach of etiquette, and Lord Morton realises what he has done and gives a small regretful cry. 'Oh!' he says, shuffling backwards. 'Beg pardon!' He looks to Lennox.

'Come in, Morton . . . No, you're most welcome.' Lennox waves a hand towards a bench at a nearby table. Morton bows courteously, slips into the middle of the company and takes a seat.

There is a time lapse before Darnley realises what the fury in his chest is: Morton should look to *him* for permission to enter – not just because these are his rooms, not just because of that, but because he is *the King*. He will be their King from tonight. They should all remember who is in charge here, what the plan was.

Unsure of his authority, feeling himself threatened, he reaches for his dagger, just to touch it, to comfort himself as if he's cupping his balls, but he finds it gone. He had it earlier. He knows he did.

He recalls the last time he felt powerful.

It was upstairs when they got Rizzio. Yes. He should give an order in front of everyone and then they'll see that he's in charge. He stands unsteadily and shouts to the guards to come in from the stairwell.

The Great Men of History stop talking and look up, interested but in no way bothered, as four of the guards enter through the doors.

'Get David Rizzio's body out of her rooms,' he orders. 'Take it downstairs.'

The guards leave. Darnley turns back to the company and, in the lull before the conversation restarts, they all hear the Queen pacing back and forth in her bedroom.

His wife is up there, waiting for the killers to come for her and the baby.

Then they hear the sound from the stairwell: outside the open door they hear Rizzio's bloody corpse being rolled down the stairs. It slaps heavily from stone step to stone step, losing momentum as it flops to a stop outside the door of this chamber. It sounds very wet. Darnley wants to move away from the door but thinks that would a bad thing to do, an undermining thing. He drains his drink as the guards speak quietly out on the stairs. Someone grunts with effort. A sloppy thing shifts, there is a hissing as a wet weight is dragged across the sandstone. Another grunt, a heel shoving maybe, and the body flops down the next set of stairs. Darnley imagines the smeared red carpet it leaves in its wake. He remembers what they did to David, remembers passing the red mess of him crumpled in the window recess. He didn't even look at it that closely but now he feels sick very suddenly and for no reason.

The Master of Guards comes back in alone. He sidles up to Darnley and whispers that they have done what he asked. He also tells him that the porter asked, and was permitted, to strip the fine clothes from the body.

Darnley doesn't understand why the guard is telling him this. It's a domestic detail and he's the fucking King. He wants to slap the man in the face, but the guard keeps rattling out details: Rizzio's bloody body is now naked and on display, lying over a trunk, and, per Lord Morton's order, the only dagger left in the body is Darnley's.

The guard holds his eye, bows and retreats.

Who was the guard? He was no one, a mean man of history, but he has changed the course of the night, snatched history from the hands of the Great, because on hearing this – *Lord Morton's order, only your dagger* – the horrified realisation dawns on Darnley that they are putting his hand on all the dirty business. It's a set-up. He will not be made King. That was never the plan.

He scans the room with inebriate eyes and admits it: these men don't think he's a king, they think he's an idiot. But what can he do? Over the course of the next hour he gets so drunk that he passes out on his bed and wakes at six o'clock with a start. Before he even opens his eyes he remembers what happened last night.

He sits up, pain sloshing around his head, picks his steps through the retainers sleeping on his floor and makes his way upstairs. The door is locked on the other side.

'Mary.' He daren't shout because the others mustn't know he's here. 'Mary, let me in, please, it's me. Please, Mary? Please? Let me in, let me talk to you. Mary?'

The door opens and the Queen stands there, bedraggled and red-eyed. She hasn't been to sleep yet, and she grabs his shirt and pulls him into the bed chamber. She locks the door after him and turns and cups his hands in hers and hisses angrily at her husband, 'I thought they killed you in the night.'

Darnley starts to weep, snivelling, frightened. She's glad he's not dead. She doesn't mistake him for an ally but she still holds his hands as he sinks, sobbing, to his knees. 'I'm so, so sorry. I'm sorry for last night.'

'For David?'

'For David, of course, for David.'

'He *loved* you, Henry. He loved *you*, and you let these traitors kill him. He's just a scapegoat.'

'I'm so sorry,' he laments, burying his face in her skirts. He isn't really sorry. She knows it and he knows it and if Rizzio were alive he would know it too. There is something wrong with Darnley, something missing. He has none of the finer feelings a human being has. He is a different kind of thing. 'Forgive me, Mary. Can you forgive me?'

'You only repent what causes you trouble.' She pulls her

hands away. 'You broke your oath to protect me. You lied and you'll do it again.'

'I won't.'

'I can't trust you. I don't know who I can trust now.'

'Mary, Mary . . . Listen . . . I can show you that you can trust me. I can tell you things.' He scrambles to his feet and dries his nose with his sleeve. 'They talked all night. They're planning to hold you hostage in Stirling Castle for the rest of your life. They're going to keep you there, you and the child.'

Child hostages have a special resonance in his family. They both know this.

'Not only us. They'll hold you there too.'

'I believe so.'

She watches his fine hands slapping tears from his cheeks. This is why he's here. He got a fright and he wants to change sides. 'But I can't trust you, Henry.'

'You can!' He watches the door he came through, thinking but not saying, *I can't trust them*.

Mary knows how to play him. 'No, you're a liar. Truth means nothing to you. Now, should you make some gesture to show me I can trust you—'

'Wait,' he says and pushes past her. 'Wait for me.'

He scurries down the stairwell and comes straight back holding two vellum documents roughly folded in three. He hands them to her unblushingly, smiling, and Mary thinks he looks terribly weary. She opens the documents and reads. It's the contract they all signed agreeing to this uprising, to the terms of it, detailing who is getting what, and it has a list of signatures of everyone involved and their respective seals.

Now she knows exactly who can be trusted and who can't. Now she knows what they want.

'You *lied* to me,' she says.

Darnley has no defence but says very quietly, 'I can lie just as well to them.'

Proclamations and Apparitions

All day Sunday, frail and hungover, Darnley does what he is told by the Great Men.

He proclaims Parliament officially dissolved. Anyone who came to Edinburgh to attend Parliament – the prelates, the earls, the lords and barons, commissioners and anyone with them – must leave the city within the next three hours or risk being arrested and forfeiture of their life, lands and goods.

There is a sudden exodus of visiting dignitaries; they gather their servants and vassals and grooms and maids and wives and mistresses and children, their horses and carriages and cartloads of furnishings, pack up their city lives and leave.

The city is deathly quiet.

No one is charged with contravention of this order and Edinburgh is a small place. It would be impossible to hide. Everyone knows something sinister is happening. A man was found covered in blood standing by a priest's bed last night, laughing. He has been arrested and thrown into gaol. He won't stop screaming. Henry Yair's maniacal cries rattle through the silent closes and the shuttered mansions of the visiting rich.

Darnley makes a second declaration: the Exiled Lords are no longer being charged with treason and their estates will not be confiscated. He declares that they can safely return to Scotland without fear of arrest or prosecution.

They're actually already in Edinburgh, most of them, hiding in different houses around the city, waiting for this pronouncement.

From the houses of allies and family and friends, the Exiled Lords come out of the shadows.

They meet each other.

They greet each other.

They're seen walking in the streets. For the conspirators, everything is working out.

Old and Pointless and Carrying a Piss Pot

On Sunday, at lunchtime, Mary starts to miscarry. She doubles over in pain and cries out, and no one is surprised. Pregnancy is ill understood but what everyone does know is that pregnant women die all the time. Babies not carried to full term die, and any complication or shock or mild infection can kill both mother and child. Birth defects are caused by 'maternal impression': a pregnant woman experiencing a shock can change the shape of the child she is carrying. A loud noise heard during gestation can cause deafness in a child. A rearing horse can cause cleft lip. The murder of a servant, an attack by eighty men and a bloodthirsty coup? That will surely bring the death of one or both.

The conspirators don't trust Mary's own midwife.

They're worried she will convey messages from the Queen to her loyalists. They send her one of their own.

This midwife visits the Queen and reports back: Mary is definitely not faking. If they want mother and child to survive, they have to release her right now.

They discuss it in the King's chamber. They won't release her. They won't change her conditions. They won't let her see her apothecary. They don't care if she sees the pregnancy to term or dies. And now they are all calculating the consequences of her dying.

In 1566, a miscarriage at six months usually means the death of the mother. Everyone is thinking about the future.

No queen, no heir, no opposition.

Mary fakes a miscarriage, on and off, for six hours and Lady Huntly stays by her side the whole time.

'Scream,' she whispers into Mary's ear and she does.

The conspirators let her stay near the Queen because she's old and pointless and she probably hates Mary more than anyone. No threat there.

'Hold your back with two hands and writhe,' instructs Lady Huntly and Mary does it and Lady Huntly cries out herself: 'Oh, my poor dear! Oh, the pity of it!'

Lady Huntly weeps all day long. When anyone asks how Mary is doing, she holds her kerchief to her mouth and shakes her head and says, 'My poor lady!'

They think it means that Mary and the baby will die. Women have experience of these things. Lady Huntly has carried twelve children herself. She'll know when it's time to cry and they're glad that she thinks this is one of those times.

Lady Huntly stays with Mary, rubbing her back, dabbing her brow and making her sip Madeira. She whispers encouragement and weeps for the younger woman's troubles. And while she weeps and wipes and murmurs comforting things to Mary, she also whispers this: *George and James got away. They've mustered a small army out in Dunbar. They'll fight for you if you can get there.*

'But why are you helping me,' asks Mary, 'after all that happened?'

Lady Huntly nods heavily, remembering her beloved son's execution, a loss that felt like being kicked in the heart by a horse. She feels an echo of that bruise every day. Then she looks up and squeezes Mary's hand, and she whispers in her ear, 'In those days I often wished for a sister to hold my hand.'

The women look at each other, and, for just a little while, neither of them need pretend they are crying. The moment passes and Lady Huntly mutters, 'Now cry out and suddenly arch your back.'

Mary does as she is told.

The only person who isn't convinced by all this is little Lord Lindsay.

He is immediately suspicious when someone tells him she is passing the child and most likely to die. It just seems too much like good luck to him because he's sober.

All day long he hangs around Mary's apartments like a bad smell, coming and going without asking permission. He's impertinent, he checks the laundry, frisks the maids, and makes people stop what they're doing to let him search them.

Lady Huntly plots all day. 'You'll need to run,' she whispers and then she calls loud, 'Poor darling!'

It's four o'clock in the afternoon and Lady Huntly declares that she needs to know whether the lady can eat something. Food arrives and Lord Lindsay is still hanging around, watching them closely, lifting bread and pawing through the dinner to make sure Mary isn't receiving secret messages smuggled in on the dinner plates.

The women try to eat around his touch as he stands by the table, rubbing himself on the corner. He's a disgusting little man.

They've had enough to eat and they want to get away from him so Mary cries out and Lady Huntly makes her retreat to the commode. This is the second turret room across from the supper room. The baby will be coming soon, she says. We had better prepare.

Once in the commode room Lady Huntly says she can bring a rope in a basket of linen and Mary can climb out of the window. It's only thirty feet to the ground.

Mary says no, she's too pregnant, it's too steep a drop and the guards are watching from the floor above.

They'll spot her immediately. What they need is for the guard to be called off. And they need to get rid of Lindsay.

'Cry out,' says Lady Huntly and Mary does as she is told. 'Oh, poor, poor child! Lord, have mercy!'

'We need the lords to think they've won,' Mary says. 'Then they'll let their guard down. Then we can get away.'

Lindsay thinks Mary and Lady Huntly are in the commode room too long. He bursts in through the door to find Mary taking a pee on her chamber pot. He's proved wrong but, determined not to show any deference, he just stands there, listening to her urinate, until she is finished. Lady Huntly lifts the chamber pot and takes it out of the room.

Lindsay is annoyed to be made to look so petty and stops the old woman. He makes her put the pot down and submit to a physical search in case she has a secret message from Mary hidden on her person. He finds nothing, waves an imperious hand, and tells her to take the piss pot away.

Lady Huntly walks, warm pee sloshing in the pot that she has covered with a cloth. She has a letter tucked deep into her bodice. It's from Mary to George and Bothwell.

Mary says she's coming to meet them. On Monday at midnight. She'll be on the road to Dunbar.

Bring an army.

Redly

Henry Yair is hoarse from screaming. His raw throat burns. Something is about to happen, something terrible. Second to second he knows this worst possible thing, unimaginable, unknowable, is about to hit him NOW. This terrible thing is going to happen NOW.

He's so afraid, his breathing is so shallow, that he can barely inhale.

He crouches in the corner of the cold cell all night, waiting, braced for impact, as Adam Black's blood dries and flakes from his hands and face.

The day sneaks up outside, noisily, redly, and Henry Yair knows nothing now. Not what is happening or where he is or where he's been or why. All he can think of is trampled meat and how glad he will be when this life is over.

He is in Hell.

The Price of Tights

Darnley has convinced the conspirators that Mary, who has been miscarrying and dying inch by inch all day long, will sign their pardons. She will ratify Protestantism as the official religion of the country. She will grant him the Crown Matrimonial. She has been in convulsions again all day, racked with birthing pains, attended by stupid old Lady Huntly. The whole matter will soon be settled.

On Monday evening, a full delegation assemble in the audience chamber and kneel grudgingly before their wincing Queen. Darnley stands by her side, looking even more pleased with himself than usual.

Mary holds her side and looks terribly drawn. She can hardly look up at them, so cowed is she. She's standing in front of the statue of the Holy Virgin and the proximity does her no favours.

In the brilliant candlelight Our Lady of the Graces is relaxed and pink of cheek. Mary is taut and pale, holding her belly with one hand, the other on her side as if she has a stitch, standing stiff as if she expects excruciating pain to hit her at any moment.

She starts to make an announcement but has to stop to catch her breath. She tries again.

'We must find a way through the events of the past few days,' she says weakly, 'to put these things into oblivion. We must find a way to bring peace into the Commonwealth for all of us. These events, these doings, they speak of a heartsore people who need heard . . .' She bends back very slightly and whispers something to Darnley.

Darnley addresses the delegation with a warm smile. 'Gentlemen, you have won. My Queen is feeling unwell and must take to her chamber but she will meet your demands. Please have them transcribed, and when she is well enough, later this evening, she will sign a document to this effect. You have my word.'

At this the men in the room smile. They're absolutely delighted. They're relieved it's all over.

'You have my word' means something at this time. It's almost legally binding, but Darnley is lying to these men; he is oath breaking and acting in bad faith. Mary wouldn't do this, but she is asking Darnley to do it. His reputation is already worthless.

Mary is feeling a lot of things this evening, in front of

these men. She is puffing and holding herself but she's not feeling anything in her belly. She is feeling disgusted by these men who killed sweet Davie, a man worth ten of any one of them. She is sorrowing for their souls: she knows they are going to Hell and that Calvinism is a passing fad that fools men into thinking they can pick and choose how to serve God. She is horrified that these men have no honour and don't even feel the need to pretend they do.

But she doesn't make any of these feelings known. She holds her belly and keens softly, as if she is trying not to make too loud a noise. She looks to the door, about to suggest they go, but she hears a cry from the back of the assembly. One man, Lord Moray, jumps to his feet and curses. He slaps at his knees and stamps and tells a servant to get him a cloth at once. Then he tuts and slaps his legs again.

The people near him are grinning.

'What is it?' whispers someone near the front.

'Got David Rizzio's blood all over his brand-new velvet hose.'

'Oh shit.' Fancy tights are very expensive.

'Blood? That's never coming out.'

From all the way across the room Mary can see the red splatters on the bright yellow fabric, and then she sees the deep pool of blood on the floor under the window.

She starts to cry. She can't stop herself. She covers her face and moans very quietly, 'He was my dear friend.'

This shames the men. They stop laughing and wish someone would get this girl out of here. They remember the night and the stabbing and they're a little bit embarrassed now. They went a bit mad that night. They can't stop thinking about it.

Suddenly Mary grips her side and cries out. Lady Huntly rushes out from the bed chamber and holds her up as her legs buckle.

Even this elicits no pity from the triumphant men.

Moray with the bloody leg stands tall and, down through the pages of history, he declares to the company: 'The loss of one mean man is of less consequence than the ruin of many lords and gentlemen.'

Mary is helped from the room by Darnley and Lady Huntly. They don't quite know what to do until Lord Darnley returns, reiterating that the Queen has decided to forgive them everything. She just wants this to be over. If they draw up the paperwork, she'll sign it. They have his word.

The Queen is as good as dead. The baby is dead. Darnley has the crown but in name only. The Lords control everything. They are to have pardons signed by the Queen for what they did to David Rizzio and all their lands and goods will be given back to them.

They have turned the tide, these Great Men of History. The sow will sign. Now it's just a matter of waiting. They draw up the statement, sign their own names and give it to Darnley to hand to the Queen in between her death pains.

And then they decide to go out for dinner to celebrate their great success.

❦

Mary rides ahead of Darnley and the others through the empty city streets. She is cloaked and her horse's hoofs are muffled with sack cloth. It has been raining, and the wettened buildings glower, darkened. The streets smell fresh and sour, the smoothed wet cobbles glint silver.

Lord Darnley can see her very clearly, and though her hood is up, he can tell from her straight back and high chin that she is exhilarated. He is wearing a cloak too, but he is horrified. He's left his father back in the Palace.

'I can't leave him here,' he whined to Mary as they slipped out through the wine cellar. 'They'll kill him.'

'Then they'll kill him,' Mary had replied, tugging at his arm. 'Stay and they'll kill both of you.'

She needs him to admit paternity of the baby when it comes. He knows that. That's why she's taking him. Not because she loves him. She doesn't love him at all.

Darnley knows his father would leave him if the roles were reversed – he knows that – but he always flattered himself into thinking he might not have done to his father what he now has. He's no different, no better than the most malevolent person he knows.

He remembers Davie: shirtless, sleeping, eyelashes as thick and long as a cow's, lush lips parted. Rizzio at tennis, watching as Darnley pretended to serve an invisible ball, his eyes smiling at Darnley's stupid joke. He killed him for no benefit. He didn't think he could do that to his father.

He looks up and realises that he has never seen the city so quiet, so pregnant, so hollow. They ride through rain-washed black streets until they reach open country and then they give the horses their heads, Mary galloping so fast she looks like a child overcome with the sheer joy of riding.

Ten miles away, George Huntly and James, Earl of Bothwell, are waiting in the dark, watching the road for their future.

Here Is a Man in a Hood with a Knife

❧

One late afternoon · May, 1566
A scaffold in Edinburgh

Henry Yair stands on a platform looking down at a large crowd. The afternoon sun is behind him and he can see their faces very clearly but thinks they probably can't see him because they're squinting. He fixes his eyes on a woman and a man, quite young, sweethearts maybe; they're holding hands. They look so concerned. Perhaps they're worried about something. He tries to nudge the man beside him to get him to look at them too but finds his hands are bound together behind his back.

Yair has been seeing apparitions in the night. Sometimes

they frighten him, these grey and green things, shifting things going quickly back and forth. Sometimes he watches them objectively because he's too tired. Sometimes he really sees what is there. Sometimes that is worse.

Standing next to him, his gallows brother, is Thomas Scott, the Perth man with the smashed-in nose. Scott is the Sheriff. Ruthven's man too. Yair smiles at him, thinking how nice it is that they are both Ruthven's men, but Scott is crying really loudly.

There are two other men up here with them, richer men. Lairds, Yair thinks. He looks at them in their fine clothes and sees they are Mowbury and Harlow. They were there that night. He saw them stab David Rizzio. He saw Harlow lift a chair and Mowbury turn towards a door and reach for the handle. He recalls these meaningless snippets of action: a man lifting a chair. He never put it down. Is it down yet? Is he still there, holding that chair high? No, he is here with Yair. Perhaps another man, same as this man here, is back there, back then, still holding that chair? Yair's memories are fractured and have no meaning. Time slides into other times yet he knows he saw these things. Mowbury and Harlow – lairds, both – lifting a chair and turning to a door.

But Mowbury and Harlow are being kept away from Scott and Yair. The lairds are all the way over the other side and they are not dirty like him and Scott.

Scott looks terrible. Yair has never seen Scott from the

side before. The bridge of his smashed nose is completely gone and – it's amazing! – he can see the tears rolling down Scott's far cheek as well as the one near to him. That's how flat his nose is. It's not in the way at all. Scott has lost some teeth recently. His chin is bloody, his gums all raggedy.

A man walks forward to the crowd and shouts things. *By order of Lord Darnley . . . David Rizzio . . . Murder . . . These men before you here held . . . Royal pardon . . . Mowbury and Harlow to be released . . . Per justice.*

Justice? Yair grins at Scott. There were hundreds of them there that night. There's only four of them standing here. That's funny if nothing else. Morton and Ruthven and all of them, and now four. Yair smiles at the crowd, at the couple, but no one smiles back.

He tries to laugh but he's been shouting so much his voice is hoarse and he can only squawk a *haw-haw*.

The two Lairds are led from the scaffold, helped down the steps to the street below, and the eyes of the young couple follow them. The crowd parts to let the Lairds through, keeping their eyes down. They seem ashamed to have witnessed the Lairds' pardon, as if they might get into trouble for having seen the men there. They turn back and look up at Yair and Scott.

Suddenly there's a hooded man and a minister in a long grey cassock reading a prayer book.

Yair has attended executions many times, but this crowd seem all wrong. This feels different. They aren't jeering the way they usually do. They're just standing there, arms by their sides, looking from one to the other, expressionless faces, heads jerking like pigeons.

He's not sure what's going on.

The shouting man says other things. *Words . . . By order of . . . Upon the night . . . Did wilfully . . . And there did . . . Father Adam Black.*

Yair brightens at the mention of Father Black. He knows that name. He smiles, remembering his funny way of walking, a hobbling and a rolling of a lame knee to propel himself forward, as if he were stepping over something. Getting around something.

Praying is going on near him, incantations, but that's a waste of time because God hates him and Yair knows that. And now the crowd are making a sound, a coo and yelp of surprise as a rope is pulled down over his neck. It sits heavily on his clavicle, resting there. He can't stop thinking about it sitting on his bones but is distracted by Scott crying loudly next to him, open-mouthed, stringy slabbers falling from his mouth onto his shirt front.

They put a rope on Scott too, and through a smog of psychosis, Yair is suddenly aware of where they are and what is being done.

Scott is asked if he wants to speak. He shakes his head. They don't ask Yair to speak but he wants to. He babbles his panic in loud, loud sounds, keeping the noises going as they push him to the edge of the platform. He raises his voice to the crowd.

I AM MAN, he tells the sky and the couple and the swirling buildings and the green air. A wind picks up suddenly, stealing his voice and carrying the earthy smell of horse as the ground beneath him disappears.

It is white, this place, a comfortable nothing, he thinks.

A sudden rush of blinding pain roars into his head and he tries to sit up, gulping in air through his massively swollen tongue.

The crowd are calling, screeching, singing, some of them, and the pain in his head is so bad that he needs to stop the light burning into his eyes, just cover his eyes, but his hands don't work. His shoulders are stuck. He can't see the crowd, just sky, and he cannot move.

Here is a man in a hood with a knife.

And the man reaches down and takes hold of Yair's cock and balls quite gently. A finger slips on the soft underside of his balls and it feels loving.

Yair laughs until the man slices them off. The crowd jeer. The hood holds them up to show Henry Yair his own sweet cock and balls that he loved all his life. Pain cascades through Yair's body, sweeping him in and out of life, in and out of the white pain in his head.

Yair looks up and he sees his own sweet cock held high above him in the sky by a bloody hand and then—

Claret on a Silver Slipper

On the morning of the christening of their son, James VI, Mary, Queen of Scots and Lord Darnley, the King Consort, have this exchange.

'You need to come to the christening, Henry. You need to own him publicly. People need to know he's your son.'

'No, no. I shan't come.' Henry is even more drunk than usual. He often is these days. His eyes are sliding around as he tries to focus and keep his knees from buckling. She wishes he'd sit down. She's worried he'll fall on the baby.

'Henry' – she doesn't even sound angry any more, just exhausted – 'he will not be safe if you don't admit him as your son.'

'Oh, really?' He is slurring badly.

They both know this about their son.

'Well, maybe I don't want to be a father.'

'It's a bit late for that,' she says.

'You may have fooled me,' he says, pouring a cup of wine and missing the glass, spilling it over the stone floor. 'Oh.' He steps a toe in the wine and it soaks into his slipper. 'I didn't even want it. What would I be . . . ? Want a son? It might not even be mine.'

He swings around and looks at her as if he has said something so witty that he has even surprised himself.

Mary isn't listening. She is looking at the red claret soaking into the tip of his silver velvet slipper. She's thinking about David Rizzio, remembering her friend: *Tell me this*, he said. *What is the sweetest portion of music you ever heard? Everyone must answer.*

Darnley sees the expression on her face, the profound sadness in her eyes and follows her gaze to his toe. It takes a moment for him to remember the bloody yellow hose, but when he does, he turns to her accusingly.

'Well, how am I supposed to know the boy isn't the Italian's?'

Mary looks at Baby James. 'You think he might be Davie's child?'

'Don't know,' mutters Darnley.

She holds up the little baby suckling on her fingertip. He has a frizz of ginger hair and skin as pale as a bright new moon. 'You think this is Davie's baby?'

Darnley shrugs and slurs, 'Who knows? I know this much: I can't be his father. I can't.'

He's right. He won't be the baby's father. He'll be murdered in two years. He won't live long enough to be a father to anyone.

Traditionally Associated with Mary, Queen of Scots

What happened to Mary is so frightening that she never goes back after she leaves Holyrood with Darnley that night. She shudders at the memory of those rooms.

The doors to her apartments slowly close. They stay shut for over two hundred years. The entire floor is abandoned. There are no Queen's apartments at Holyrood or anywhere else in Scotland because Mary is captured and taken to England. She is held prisoner until her execution on 8 February 1587. The next Scottish Queen doesn't want to visit her rooms in Holyrood either because of what had happened that mad weekend.

It is an ignominious memory, baffling to an audience

more distant from the Reformation and the binary mindset that framed everything as a clash of absolutes. A pall of collective shame falls over the lovely rooms and the memory of what happened there.

A Keeper of the Palace of Holyrood is appointed. It's a hereditary post. They live in the Palace, and Mary's apartments come to be used as a storage area for unwanted furniture. Old beds and cabinets, tables and commodes are stacked and abandoned, the space filled with all the things no one knows what to do with. Dust gathers and moths thrive. Mice nest in the dark corners. Broken chairs and woodwormed wardrobes sag.

Day follows day, season follows season.

After a hundred years, a small windowpane in the bed chamber snaps in the cold and falls out, but it is behind a tall cabinet and no one notices. The rain gets in, unseen, for decades. The wooden floor gets wet and swells up and rots. In the summer mould forms and makes the apartment smell of sweet mildew. Things fall apart, dovetailed joints snap, unique and priceless bits of furniture slowly melt into one another.

It takes two hundred years to lift the stink, and, when it is finally long enough in the past to morph into a romantic tale, it is the English who cherish the story of the beautiful, bullied Queen of Scots.

Walter Scott's *The Abbot* is published in 1820, six years into his stratospheric writing career, and revives interest in Mary. Privileged Scott fans use their influence to inveigle a visit to Mary's apartments. They come into her audience chamber, take the passage to her bed chamber. They stand in the door by the little supper room, go into the commode room, take the back stairs down to Darnley's suites and the grand staircase back up. But they are disappointed. They find the rooms crammed with broken dusty crap. Damp mouldy things. You have to sidle through, and the floor is so rotten it doesn't feel safe.

Still, relics of Mary are much sought after and they take things away anyway, supposing them mementos, not knowing they are mostly junk that had been dumped in her rooms after she left. Eventually no one knows what did and didn't belong to Mary, Queen of Scots.

The apartment is ignored and then restored with the heavy-handed vigour of Victorian builders. The rotten floorboards are ripped out and replaced, the whole floor raised by six inches.

In the twenty-first century, her rooms have glass display cases with many items carefully labelled 'Traditionally Associated with Mary, Queen of Scots'. The curators are too honest to misdate them. Many were made long after her death. The curators are too honest to misdate them.

A brass plaque is screwed into the wooden panelling of a window nook in the old audience chamber.

It's very low down. You have to stoop to read the words.

THE BODY OF

DAVID RIZZIO

was left here after his murder

in Queen Mary's supper room,

9th March, 1566.

And the floorboards below it are stained red.

Blood, traditionally associated with Mary, Queen of Scots.

Acknowledgements

I'd like to thank Jamie Crawford for commissioning this, for sending the first draft back with a resounding 'meh' and forcing me to make it better. He always does that and he's always right, which is intensely aggravating. Also, many, many thanks to Alison Rae for edits, reshapes and cobble-dating and to Katie Buckhalter of the Royal Collection Trust for so kindly arranging a private tour of the apartments.